Sweet Redemption

by

Moody Holiday

Pretty Paper Press, LLC

Sweet Redemption
By Moody Holiday

Copyright © 2003 Moody Holiday

Second Printing-June, 2004
Book design by Sisters' Computer Design

ISBN: 0-9746315-1-5

The MHoliday design is a trademark of the author.

Printed In The U.S.A.

In loving memory of my sister

Lori's Love

She turned the rope for me to jump,
Over and under the Brooklyn sun.
Didn't wait until mom got home,
kissed my boo boos when we were alone.
Topped it off with a glass of ice tea.
My big sister, sweet as can be.

Played with dolls till the age of twelve,
Wrote short stories and painted our nails.
Fought over Michael and handsome Billy Dee.
"I'll marry them both," she retorted with glee.

A pillar of strength, a source of hope,
Lori sips tea with angels, I write to cope.

Reaching for the sky,
slowly closing my eyes,
my fingertips reach up to heaven.
"Lori, I need a hug."
A warm breeze coated with the serenity of the sun,
embraces me with love.

Always with me,
forever by my side,
Lori's love never died.

Table of Contents

Sweet Redemption

Sweet Redemption,
dark of night.
Secret whispers,
life takes flight.
Surrender to sin,
bury the past.
A predator's corpse,
a winding path.

Serene in beauty,
majestic in awe.
Audible whispers,
a fatal flaw.

The sweetest baby born for him.
Cinnamon savior, handsome as sin,
sweeps the fair maiden,
Sweet redemption begins...

Issues

Alex Julian Foster, the man of my dreams, first lover and fiancé. What more could a girl like me ask for and was I deserving of such a good man? From his soft kisses to his powerful hands, I didn't want to leave his embrace for fear he would never return.

The holiday weekend of making love for the very first time left us as the Tuesday morning sun arose. Alex had to return to his regular routine as a police officer for the town of Lakewood. As a result, I woke up alone, nestled under a thin yellow sheet surrounded by empty silence.

As the warmth of sunlight began to pierce through the blinds, I rolled over to look at the clock on the nightstand. A small note on Alex's pillow caught my attention first. In anticipation for reading his heart felt words, I sat up and carried my feet to the floor. The note read, *"Sleep becomes you Shanelle. Get pretty for me so we can tell my family the good news. After we leave my parents' house tonight, we're going to North Orange to tell your parents."*

In an instant, my mind went completely blank as the clock stopped ticking and the world's orbit ceased. The delicate note was set free from the nerve endings in my hand. Fear and anxiety slowly seeped into my blood stream. I opened my mouth and mimicked the written words in slow motion. *"Tell your parents the good news."*

I watched the note fall to the hardwood floor like a mature leaf on an autumn day. Although it possessed no beauty or color, it rippled to the ground with such declaration that I could not fathom an outcome except sadness and shame. My face contorted into a state of confusion as I thought to myself, *"How could such a tiny piece of paper contain such a powerful message?"*

Destructive contemplation set in as the ball of my foot began to push the note towards the darkness beneath the bed. A soft creak in the floor quickly changed my course of action as I listened for Alex. My foot stopped moving as he walked towards me. I bit my lip wondering how I could hide the tiny message. The floor below me quickly changed into black shiny shoes. Alex lifted my chin up slowly and announced himself, unaware that his note was resting on the floor.

"Hey, you finally decided to wake up sleepy head?" The smile on Alex's cinnamon face was confident. The love we made over the weekend sent me into endless dream sleep and he knew I was finally his with a sealed engagement ring on my finger.

My body relaxed just by the sound of his voice. It had just the right base and on any given day, all I could do was melt. A response flowed from my mouth as if I swallowed a succulent truth serum. "Good morning," I replied, as my chin continued to rest in his mighty hands.

Alex continued to stare at me as he caressed my face with a caring smile. I contemplated pulling him on top of me, but his note diminished my need to make love to him. I didn't want to lose focus with my plan to destroy it, but I was fading fast as he looked at me. My heart started to beat slowly from his touch as his eyes shifted to the floor. Alex bent down and retrieved the note from under my foot as a tiny voice buried deep inside of me whispered, *"You're busted Shanelle, he's a cop remember? You can't get shit past him girl."*

I quickly accepted ownership of the note by concentrating on the things that pleased him. I looked into his eyes and said, "If sleep becomes me, I'll sleep for you all day." I didn't want to entertain anything else and even if I tried, Alex's intentions were quickly coming to the surface. I wanted to paralyze the tiny piece of paper by snatching it from his grip and crushing it with my hand. I did not want him to know I was desperate and afraid.

I continued to look him in the eyes while he began to physically connect with me. Alex was consistent in his need to touch me as he played with my untamed hair. He pinched my earlobe and said, "You can't sleep all day Shanelle, we've got too much to do." Alex took his car keys out of his pocket and whipped them around his pointer finger. There was no sense in distracting him because he was completely focused on two things, going to work and spreading our good news.

Alex brought the dismal message into reality again as he sat on the bed and asked, "So, what about the note?" He handed it to me by placing it in the palm of my hand. I looked at the note and prayed for a formulated answer, but it never came. Thank goodness Alex exercised patience on a daily basis. He was rarely at a loss for words, but his actions commanded an answer. Alex cleared his throat and sat next to me. The weight of his body on the mattress gave way and pressed our shoulders together. Alex said nothing, but he crossed his legs in a commanding gesture. He began to retie his shoes by carefully pulling the laces tight in a quick and swift motion. His grip forced the strings into a tight snapping sound that immediately caught my attention. We stared at each other and after a momentary pause Alex said, "Look Shanelle, you owe it to your parents. Let's get this over with and make peace."

My face became reflective as I stared at our photograph filled bedroom. There were enough pictures of us to occupy myself and avoid his answer. To make good use of his time, Alex stood up and adjusted his bulletproof vest. He continued to stare at me and methodically adjusted his belt. Then he took a deep breath and paused. My eyes shifted in his direction, but I couldn't look at him. Even if he was waiting for a response, I could not speak. Alex began to massage my shoulders and said, "Ok Shanelle, we'll talk about it at lunch."

It was the break I was looking for as I finally looked at him in pure relief. Alex's love for me led him straight to the floor and on his knees. He spread my legs with his large hands and tucked his massive frame into my body. A warm embrace soothed me for the moment and eased my worry. My response to him was rhythmic as I held him tight. Alex nestled his head in my breasts and pacified himself before he left for work. He also whispered words to me for reassurance.

"Baby girl, you're going to be fine. I'm here for you, and I'm not going anywhere." Alex took a deep breath as he pressed my back closer into his frame. I was comforted by his touch as I rested my chin on top of his head. No matter how comforting it was, our embrace did little to diminish my mental anguish. I thought to myself, "Derrick used to call me baby girl too." I also wondered if Alex thought I was a child in his eyes. More troubling to me was the family meeting on Cresent Avenue and the voices that began to carry me away again. The Big One spoke first.

"*I hope Mrs. Viv takes a shot at the back of her big ass head, that's always a good laugh.*"

The Little Meek One replied, "*No, no way, she's going to make her clean out the fridge.*"

The Big One chuckled and replied, "*Better yet, wait till dear daddy sees her new ring.*"

I shut my eyes tight and wished them all away. I needed to soothe my own sense of worry so I began to rub Alex's back in large circular patterns. Ponder forced me to wonder, "Why are they so chatty today?"

Even though Alex could barely feel my touch through the weighted material, the sensation always relaxed him before he went to work. I was glad he had to wear his vest because I could not imagine life without him on any given day. My love for Alex was so great that I was in no position to let him go to my parents' house like a sitting duck. I thought to myself, "What are you going to tell him?" I certainly wasn't looking for his pity. I wanted to forget Cresent Avenue and all the horrors inside. Steven's rampages and small dark closets created festered images in my head that were hard to think away. The note only brought the images back to the surface and I was determined to suppress them. Alex continued to nestle in the warmth of our bodies as I rubbed his head. Small bouts of calm became me as I settled my resolve. I decided to accept the terms of his note for love. I thought to myself, "He doesn't know Shanelle…he doesn't have to know about the voices or the closets."

Realizing that duty called, Alex snapped out of his trance and stood up. He sighed out loud and said, "Baby, I'll call you during my break." Then he grabbed my hand and thought out loud, "Oh yeah, I'm definitely coming home for lunch."

The tone in his voice excited me as I let go of his hand to hug him goodbye. I asked, "What do you want to eat?"

His response was devilish and smooth. He pulled me into his frame and said, "Hmm, let's see, how about you and some of that cantaloupe you picked up the other day?" He certainly had a way with words and I fell for him every time. I looked up at him and said, "Keep it up and you'll be late for work officer."

Alex looked at his watch and considered my seductive offer. "Sounds tempting, but I'll hold out till lunch time."

One last hug satisfied us as Alex headed for the door. I laughed at the thought of his constant affection, but I knew that he was quite serious in his need for me. There was no way I was going to disappoint his desire to make love at noon. Alex was so determined in everything he said and everything he wanted, especially me. After making him wait so long, there was no way I could say no to him. I tiptoed behind him like a little school girl as his handcuffs and keys jingled in tune. As we stood at the door, Alex swept my lips with his thumb. The look in his eyes said it all as he spoke to me. "I love you girl."

I locked the door behind him as the sound of Alex's whistling disappeared through the secondary entrance. My need for him forced me to the window to watch him leave the complex. Alex took his grand walk of fame by waving to the neighbors and joking about the weather. He looked so happy getting into his car and yes, so incredibly handsome. The tips of my fingers adjusted the blinds for the right shade of sunlight through the window. My other hand stroked the places that Alex aroused. As he pulled out of the complex, I walked away from the window and stared at our apartment. The warmth of his touch was still with me as goose bumps rose upon my skin. I thought to myself, "Three challenges face me today." One was more complex than the next. The first was preparing a love-induced afternoon with Alex during his lunch hour. That was easy to prepare for including fresh fruit, scented oils, one of his undershirts tied into a midriff and black see through panties. The second assignment was easy. With Alex by my side, my engagement ring and Alex's assertiveness would take over and leave me in a relaxed frame of mind. I was comfortable in his mother's house and hoped that she would prepare a nice meal for everyone to enjoy. Thinking of the third task made me uneasy. My stomach began to twist and turn in a tug of war as I rubbed my belly with my bare hands. The return home to Crescent Avenue in North Orange was an outcome I could not ignore or predict. "Shit," was my first response. "Damn you Steven," was my second, as I rested my fingertips on my temples.

The pleasure of Alex's touch left my body as soft murmurs began. I began to press deeper into my temples and looked around. Among the quiet walls and hollow doors, my world felt occupied by demons and voices, some strange, others were as witty as Richard Pryor. I did not want to know them, but they escaped and found a way to find me in my new world with Alex. Time could only contemplate their intentions.

Voices

I needed to get ready for Alex's lunch break so I closed the blinds and turned off the TV to prevent any distractions. Mental interruptions plagued my mind in various forms. Questions, doubts and rhetoric fused together like a convention and I could not get in to settle them down. I walked into the bathroom and took off my clothes from the previous night. My arms began to itch as processed goose bumps permeated my skin with thoughts of returning home.

"I don't want to go back there, please leave me alone, I'm fine just where I am, everything is clean now Mama, leave me alone Steven, help me Daddy. Who are you Shanelle?"

The audible words began to settle down into a small whisper, but they wouldn't go away. I tried to escape into a fantasy flight, but I couldn't get it off the ground. As each murmur continued, I closed the door in haste to hear the intruders. I strained my face to concentrate, but the words were impossible to understand. I stared into Alex's bathroom mirror and pressed my nose gently against the glass. My eyes shifted to the left and then to the right. I didn't see anything unusual. I exposed my left eye by pulling down the skin underneath and my eye looked clear. The right eye produced the same result as I stood on the cold ceramic tile floor listening to the confused voices. In order to distract myself, I decided to shift my concentration to a physical task. The sight of my toothbrush began to appeal to my taste buds. Reaching for the toothbrush was at best the resemblance of a slow motion picture. My goose bumps began to disappear as I picked up the toothpaste with my other hand. I tried to hold on tightly to prevent my hands from trembling, but there was little I could do. I looked in the mirror and noticed small beads of sweat at the temple of my hairline. The need to focus forced me to look down and meticulously spread the toothpaste on the brush. My hands began to shake as I tried to talk my way through the process.

"Stay cool Shanelle, you're okay, take deep breaths and focus."

The calm of my voice brought me closer to the creamy texture. It was blue mint with stripes of white and red gel. The substance was too alluring to waste on brushing, so I held my head back slowly and began to squeeze the creamy substance into my mouth. It was cool and creamy going down my throat like the frozen yogurt machines at the mall. I looked up at the swirling texture and forced it down my throat with hard concentrated swallows. The sensation overwhelmed me so much that I began to sweat in my palms and under my armpits. It happened so quickly that I didn't realize I swallowed the entire tube. I forced the remaining toothpaste out of the tube by curling it down tightly like a boa constrictor forcing the life out of its prey. The creamy droplets that followed were escorted to the back of my throat with my pointer finger. My stomach began to feel full, but not enough to satisfy my need for more. I walked into the kitchen without conscious or clothes. The world stopped moving for me as I reached for the peanut butter in the kitchen cabinet. In a gothic trance, I returned to the bathroom and closed the door to my sanctuary. I washed my hands without toweling them off and dipped my right hand into the plastic jar.

My precision was perfect as I scooped out a handful of peanut butter. I shoved the substance down my throat bringing immediate relief to my tortured existence. It was hard to swallow, but I was able to eat half of the twelve-ounce jar without feeling nauseous. The sensation of feeling full calmed me down and settled the whispers in my head forcing them into silence. It was impossible to force the peanut butter back up and this was one time that I needed it to stay there. The voices were much too powerful today.

Remnants of my demise were stuck to the tile walls as I stood up. The immediate head rush sent me back to the floor to avoid a dizzy spell. I wiped the sweat off my brow and used some toilet tissue to clean my face. The shower was my next release. I sat on the floor of the tub as the water pulsated into my open mouth. The feeling increased my need to relax as I looked at my swollen stomach .

"You look so fat you fucking bitch, you need to go on a diet, look at you."

I shut my eyes to block out Steven's voice, but it was controlling and persistent.

"He is going to find out how fat you are and leave you bitch."

The internal voice continued with more voices from my past. I covered my ears with my hands, but it served little purpose as they continued.

"Shanelle, you're a disgrace, the bottom of the barrel and you won't amount to anything."

"Good afternoon Sister Rose."

"Good afternoon girls, you may be seated. Before we begin morning prayers, I want to remind all of you that in order to be accepted, you cannot have psychotic siblings. Surely the demons will take you next, making it impossible to get ahead in life. Shanelle, please leave and take your book bag with you, we don't allow knives in our school."

"But I need it for protection Sister; I'm going home to show my father my new ring. Hopefully my brother won't

try to steal it. It will also block me against any punches thrown my way."

My courageous plea for help did little to stop them as rapid breathing took over. I placed my head into the shower stream and began to moan.

"*That's it Shanelle, good girl, no more crying, we prefer soft moaning. That way, no one can hear us. That's it, take your time, we love you when you're weak.*"

I stood up to my aggressors this time because I couldn't take it anymore. I slammed my fists on the bathroom tile and said, "Whoever you are, stop the bullshit, I've had enough!"

I began to lather my washcloth with soap, rethinking what went wrong. The peanut butter vice used to work all the time, but had little to no effect today. I balled my fists up tight and placed them at my temples to hush away the noise, but it didn't work. I clenched my teeth as I began to curse Alex's decision. "This is not going to work Alex. I hate you for doing this to me!" My breath escaped so quickly that I began to choke and uncontrollably babble to myself. "Mama is going to be furious, Daddy is going to call me a sugar shack whore and Steven is going to put an end to my misery."

Drool escaped my mouth and landed into the shower stream as my tirade continued. "I don't care what you think of me Steven and if I never see you again, it'll be good for me!"

My hands rested on my hips as the vocal release settled me down. I pushed my hair back and let the stream pulsate onto my face. Everything started coming back into focus as I slowly gasped for air. My tantrum had a simple conclusion. Pleasing Alex meant going home. Losing him was unacceptable. With little or no choice, it had to be done.

The shampoo sat in eyesight as I poured it into my hair shaft. The massage made me more alert, even defensive about what could happen tonight. I was so deep in thought I could barely hear the phone ringing. But when I did, I jumped out of the shower so fast I almost slipped on the floor. I answered it dripping wet as the soapy residue trickled down the side of my face. The tone in my voice was riddled with frustration.

"Hello."

Alex paused at first and then said, "Hey baby girl, what took you so long?" He didn't sound worried but awfully curious.

"I'm sorry," I said, as I paused to catch my breath. "I was in the shower and I couldn't hear it with the door closed."

"Oh," Alex replied, "Are you okay?"

Before I could think of an answer, a radio dispatch came in from the patrol car loud and clear. "All units respond to a 302 at the corner of Chestnut and Amsterdam."

Alex didn't hesitate to end our conversation. "Got to go babe, I love you."

I chimed in, but I could barely get my message out. "I love…"

The dial tone blared into the earpiece as I stood dripping wet. Loving him the way I did forced me to speak to him even though he was out of earshot. "I love you Alex, be safe."

Loneliness overwhelmed me as I walked back to the shower. Nothing seemed to matter whenever I spoke to him. I prayed that he was ok and that no harm would come to him on the streets. My worry for Alex was so great that it was just the right trick to settle the voices. I pictured his face in his patrol car talking to his partner Jack. It comforted me to know that I could conjure up images of him until he got home. After my shower, I went to the bedroom and turned on the TV to keep me company until he came home. I toweled dried my hair and turned on Eyewitness News.

There was a special news report on the arrest of a reputed drug kingpin in New York who was responsible for a high distribution of crack cocaine throughout the metropolitan area. Crack was the "new" drug of choice on the street because it was cheap. It got so bad that I had to abandon the notion of going into the Village because several women were beaten with car antennas for money. For a while, New York looked like an ugly city. I worried about Alex's safety and hoped that it didn't come to New Jersey. We talked about the news all the time, but drugs and weapons was the one thing he avoided in conversation. I knew there was talk at the precinct that several officers were going to special narcotics and weapons training, but he made it his business to keep me out of the loop.

I stared at the TV and watched the kingpin walk to the white Chevy Caprice as two officers carefully lowered his head into the vehicle. A pretty Latina news reporter wrapped up the news coverage as I held the remote in my hand.

"More news at 12:00 noon, this is Carmen Rivera, reporting live from the Brooklyn Criminal Court house, back to you Bill."

I looked at the clock and turned the TV off as I jumped off the bed. With less than an hour to go, I needed to get ready for Alex. I ran around the apartment picking up various pieces of clothing and the newspaper. As I scurried past the bathroom, I suddenly remembered the remnants of peanut butter stuck to the wall. With immediate haste, I grabbed a paper towel and feverishly wiped it away.

To increase the aroma in the room, I lit some citrus candles in the bedroom and bathroom. The air conditioner needed a slight adjustment so Alex could immediately cool off once he got in the door. Those little things I did for him weren't enough, but I took pleasure in keeping his life worry free when he came home.

By noon Alex was home putting the key into the lock. A few dishes were left over, but I abandoned them as soon as he walked in the door. He was deep in thought which was unusual for him. He was usually in a good mood regardless of his day on the streets. I grabbed his wrists to get his undivided attention as he looked at me like visual eye candy.

"Hey babe, what's wrong, tough day?"

He gave me another once over from my pink toes to the top of my head and escorted me towards the bathroom.

"Yeah, it's crazy out there and the heat isn't helping."

I stopped at the bathroom door entrance and watched Alex methodically wash his hands. He dried his hands with the hand towel I gave him and started undressing. I watched him take his clothes off with complete lust in my eyes. Each layer of clothes he removed aroused me as he looked at me with piercing eyes. Placing one hand on my hip, I began to stroke my collarbone as I admired his thick frame. My eyes spoke to him as he smiled at me. He started to laugh and said, "What, tell me." I replied, "You're so damn sexy Alex, that's what." Alex laughed as he looked into the mirror to confirm my comment and said, "Yeah, well we need to do something about that."

With all of my free time, there was nothing left to do but proposition his every wish. Strain and worry left his wrinkled brow as he washed his hands again and splashed cold water on his face. Alex dried his face with his towel and looked at me again as he wiped the excess water from his chin.

"All I want is you right now Shanelle."

My eyes began to widen as he grabbed the tube of toothpaste. Suddenly his face became contorted as he asked, "What happened to the toothpaste, we just brought this tube?"

Quickly rising to the occasion, I answered him back. "Oh, I got carried away and cleaned all of my jewelry, sorry."

The officer in Alex didn't seem to care. A tiny visitor spoke to me in my left ear and said, *"You're so stupid Shanelle, Steven stole your jewelry."*

He brushed his teeth and spit into the sink without flinching. I began to worry if my lie had any impact. Alex's routine was so consistent it was easy to watch him as I learned his time saving tricks. But I could never figure out what he was really thinking. While I stared at him, I contemplated becoming a better liar to avoid going back to North Orange. Since I made one mistake with the toothpaste comment, I didn't want him to get suspicious. I abandoned further thoughts of lying to him and continued to watch his routine.

Everything Alex did was like a form of order. The way he dressed, showered and groomed himself was the stuff the Marines prepared for on a daily basis. He wiped off the countertop with a paper towel and grabbed me by the wrist.

"Take a shower with me baby, I missed you." I freed myself from his grip and kissed him while I stood on my tippy toes. He pulled me in closer to him and picked me up off the floor. I was amazed that he could pick me up so easily because at one hundred and forty pounds, I was solid. It didn't faze Alex one bit as I wrapped my legs around his waist. He leaned up against the wall as I kissed his face and then put my tongue in his mouth. Alex moaned like a bear as he whispered in my ear, "Get in the shower with me now."

At his command, I slid down, flashed him a dreamy smile and stepped in with my clothes on. There was no sense in complaining about wet hair or taking a second shower because Alex didn't give a damn. I searched his eyes for suspicion or interrogation, but there was nothing but love in his eyes. He handed me his washcloth as I washed him from head to toe. Alex ran his fingers up and around my wet tee shirt. He was so focused on teasing me that I started laughing.

"Alex stop! That tickles."

He was amused by my behavior as he popped the right seam of my panties.

I laughed out loud and said, "Keep playing, you love to waste money."

Alex grabbed the other side, popped the seam and threw my panties to the floor. His laughter was louder as he swept Kitty's curly wet hair with his hands. "Baby girl, you can buy as many panties as you want, I'll rip those too if necessary."

He turned the water off and grabbed two towels. We stepped out of the shower but never made it back to the bedroom. Alex laid me down on the bathroom floor and took small bites out of the surface of my skin. He grabbed my hand and squeezed it tight as he entered me. The pleasure of Alex in his entirety forced me to call his name as I arched my back and pushed my nails into his firm skin. Alex made love to my mind as he swept words into my ears that drove me crazy. "Being inside of you makes me whole. I love you so much girl." I bit his ear and whispered, "It's all yours baby, make me whole." Alex covered my mouth with his hand to silence me as his body tightened up and then settled back down again. "Don't talk, don't talk, that drives me crazy." I was enjoying him so much I surrendered to silence as he called my name. I stroked his back and ran my thumb across his mouth so he could take a soft bite. He lifted my leg up and kissed my calf in complete focus. He used his other hand to force Kitty into an orgasmic rush as my back arched off the floor. I called his name as he rested his muscular hand on my throat. Alex looked at me as I called his name and calmed me with a quiet kiss. Time quickly escaped us as he succumbed to our rhythms and released his seeds of life inside of me.

The bathroom floor was the perfect place to be on that muggy day. Alex was sweating profusely as he pulled me closer to him on the cold tile floor. He kissed my neck and rubbed my stomach with his hands. I knew what he was thinking, but I didn't say a word about protection. The comfort and safety of Alex's arms was all I wanted for the moment. I placed my hand on top of his hand and we rubbed my stomach together. Alex whispered in my ear, "I want a son Shanelle."

I closed my eyes and stroked his hand as he caressed my stomach. "I know Alex, I'll give you a son one day, just wait and see." He looked so happy when I said those words, but deep down inside, I knew his need was more immediate than my spoken promise. For the moment, the rush to his head was the first thing he had to deal with. I jumped up and poured him a glass of orange juice. Alex gulped it down like a mighty giant as he stared at me. After that he took a deep breath and got in the shower. As he lathered up, I wrapped myself up in a towel and kept him company while he began speaking over the noise of the shower.

"Shanelle, there was a big meeting today with some heavy hitters from the Federal Narcotic and Tactical Weapons Task Force. Captain Fisco assigned me and Jack to the Tactical Weapons Squad. Apparently a major sting is under works on your side of town. If the operation goes well, we might be assigned permanently. For now we're going to be on loan to the feds."

I sat up and looked at him through the shower door not knowing whether that was good news or bad news. Alex opened the shower door and extended his hand. "C'mon angel, get in and wash off," he said. As I stepped in, Alex turned me around and washed my back as I enjoyed the gentle scrub. When I turned around, Alex greeted me with a soapy fingertip. He decorated my nose with bubbles as I giggled and stepped aside. Alex stepped out of the shower and quickly got dressed.

After five minutes of whistling in the bedroom, Alex came into the bathroom and said, "Captain Fisco said I can take my vacation time to take care of personal business, but when I get back, I'm going to be gone for a month in Philly for special weapons training."

My heart started to race as my nerves became restless. I peeked out the shower door and said, "I won't be able to see you for a month?"

Alex sensed my worry and asked me to step out of the shower. In that short period of time, he was fully dressed in a fresh uniform except for his shoes, bullet-proof vest and shirt. He wrapped me up in a fresh towel as we walked back to the bedroom. I sat down next to him but he wasn't satisfied with the seating arrangement. He patted his lap and said, "Sit here."

I stood up and straddled his waist as the towel fell to my waist side. Alex smiled as he kissed my breasts. He pulled me in closer to him as our noses began to touch and said, "You know I love you Shanelle, right?"

My smile was met with worry, but I responded by saying, "Yes, I know."

"Good," Alex replied. "I need you to be strong for me until I get back. Don't get me wrong, I know you're strong, but it can get a little lonely sometimes."

I continued to stare at him as he looked down at my stomach. Then he hugged me and said, "Baby all I want is for you to be safe and happy. You can stay here or at my mother's house in my old room until I get back."

I rejected his idea by shaking my head as I bit my thumbnail. "Alex, everything is changing so fast, I don't even know what I'm going to do for the rest of the summer."

Alex stood up as I remained wrapped in his tight embrace. He said confidently, "Hopefully, morning sickness will set in as soon as we get back from our vacation."

I squeezed my legs tighter around his waist and grabbed his face. The morning sickness statement went right over my head. "Vacation, I've never been on vacation, where?"

Alex placed his hands under my armpits and placed me back on the floor.

"The Bahamas."

His response sent me into an immediate dance as I followed Alex to the door. "Be ready by five o'clock Shanelle and don't make anything, my mother's cooking."

I locked the door behind him and started jumping up and down again. It was a shame Alex had to go back to work, but I was glad that he left in a better mood. I started cleaning up from our interlude and wondered about our vacation and his fast promotion. The world was definitely changing and all I wanted was to see Alex safe in my arms again. I knew very little about the drug world except for the images on TV. The secrecy behind all of it seemed frightening and I wondered if he would want to stay with the task force. I didn't even know if he liked the idea and I felt stupid for not asking. I accepted everything he said without question and to be honest, it felt like the best thing to do. I didn't want him to think I was a nagging fiancée. My mind quickly shifted to the thought of the trip. "Lucky me," I thought. "Wait till Candy hears the news about our vacation." I dialed her number and breathed a sigh of relief when she picked up the phone. For once she was in the dorm room and studying for a change. Flight attendant school was going well and she was also in love. The lucky pilot was head over heels for his sweet young thing and had already taken her to two destinations in one week. She talked about her fabulous Dominican tan and was extremely delighted about my news with the exception of one thing.

"What do you mean he doesn't use a condom?"

I shrugged my shoulders and sat on the bed. "He doesn't want to use one and he made himself pretty clear Candy."

"Well I guess your going to be pretty pregnant if you keep that up, are you ready for all of that Shanelle?" There was a pause between us, but Candy continued her questioning. "Damn, that's a bit much don't you think, you're only nineteen."

I fixed the sheet on our bed and sat down. Candy was right, I was only nineteen.

"You're right Candy, but…," Candy barely let me finish my sentence. "I know I'm right. You haven't finished partying, enjoying life and figuring out who you are. Damn, we all like Alex, but the two of you need to get to know each other first and see how that shit really feels."

All I could do was sigh. She had good intentions, but there was nothing wrong with my perfect world. Candy continued.

"Shanelle, you know you're my girl, but I think you forgot about all the hopes and dreams you had about going to college and grad school. You and Derrick talked about that shit all the time. Now that you're with Alex, is your life going to be school books with a baby strapped to your hip?" She adjusted the tone in her voice after she heard me sighing.

"Damn Shanelle, at this point, we have to do what makes us happy. So if you're happy, then I'm happy for you."

I breathed a sigh of relief and gripped the phone to prevent it from falling on the floor.

"We're going to the Bahamas to get married, I don't

know the dates yet, but it would be so nice if you could join us."

Candy laughed at me and said, "Girl, you've got big dreams."

We exchanged some more pleasantries and then hung up with each other. Candy was hard on me but not for long. As long as those dreams were with Alex, I didn't give a damn.

Good News

Just like clockwork, Alex picked me up at five o'clock and we headed to his parents' house. His entire family was there to greet us at the door as his sisters pulled me into their huddle and grabbed my ring finger.

"Oh girl, it's beautiful," Mary said. She was the wise and oldest sister who always had kind words to share. I turned around to see what Alex was doing and he was busy staring into his mother's adoring eyes. She was proud as a peacock in her jeans and sweatshirt. I knew they shared secret messages but I didn't care. She was a kind woman and a good mother. I knew in my heart that Alex would be good to me just by the way he treated her. Alex cut the conversation short and announced our plans. "Listen up family, no bridesmaids and no drama for this family. I'm taking three weeks vacation to spend time with Shanelle. We're going to have a quiet ceremony in the Bahamas. You can do whatever you want when we get back, but my job is sending me to Philly for a month and I need you to look out for Shanelle."

Even though I wasn't embarrassed, there was no comfort in being smothered by a large family. My eyes shifted to the ground and when I looked up, they were all smiling at me with love and affection. Guilt set in because I wanted to shut them out of my seemingly quiet existence.

I surveyed the room and said, "I'll be fine Alex, thanks everyone for caring about me so much."

A small tear trickled down my face as Tammy, the youngest sister slid her big hips next to me and forced me closer to Alex. She wrapped her arms around me and said, "We can hang out before I start school. Don't worry Shanelle, I'm going to miss big head too."

Everyone started laughing as Alex rested his hand on top of my hand and squeezed it with assurance. I was amazed at their togetherness. Mrs. Foster smiled at all of us. There was no way the queen was stepping down from her throne, but she did allow her girls to assume responsibility every now and then. As for Alex, he controlled everything he did without fault and his father was as proud as his body could carry him. Mr. Foster stood up and extended his hand to Alex and pulled him off the couch.

"I'm proud of you son, you've done well. If you remember everything I taught you, you and Shanelle will be fine."

Mr. Foster looked at me and said, "Girl, I know there's a strong woman in there and maybe you're being too kind by not showing that side of your personality. You ought to know that we take pride in our family by doing things our way and I want you to feel the same. Don't let these girls smother you while Alex is gone. But if you want to come by and get something to eat or just talk, somebody will be right here anytime in the day or night."

More tears followed as I stood up to hug him for his southern hospitality. It felt so strange hugging Mr. Foster. He immediately made my heart ache for my father and I knew he was just an hour and a half away from me. My head turned as I continued to hug Mr. Foster. Alex was looking at the two of us with compassion. I let Mr. Foster go and walked into Alex's embrace. He whispered in my ear and said, "Let's get you home, I know you miss your family Shanelle."

Mrs. Foster handed me a tissue as I held Alex's hand in quiet reflection. There was no need to say anything more about our wedding plans. Mrs. Foster already knew Alex's plans. I'm sure he told her before he told me. By the looks of things, she was ok with it and the whole family had to follow suit. I didn't care what the plans were; I would have married Alex over a plate of black-eyed peas and rice. He was perfect given the life I left behind. More importantly, I loved him and short of the trip home, there was nothing that could stop our happiness.

Mrs. Foster asked the family to gather in prayer before we ate. She also asked God to keep us safe and fill her home with more healthy grandchildren. Alex squeezed my hand when she mentioned our future offspring. With Alex's persistence, it wouldn't be long before her wish came true.

Alex's sisters made such a fuss over me that I never had a chance to help Mrs. Foster with the dishes. I went into the kitchen to apologize, but she laughed me off as she closed the door to the dining room.

"Shanelle, you and my son have your whole lives ahead of you to make up for soiled dishes. All I know is that I have never seen him so happy." She grabbed my wrist and shook it in a loving way. "Alex can't wait to have children so you've got your work cut out. But if you can give him a son, he will be the happiest man on this earth."

I started laughing and let my guard down. "I can't even tell you how many times he has rubbed my stomach like there's already something in there."

Mrs. Foster started laughing and said, "Girl, ever since Alex was a little boy, it has been his way or the highway. He loves his family, but he's ready for his own little brood. With all these women around him, I know he is tired of periods, weddings and proms. In fact, his nephews are the only ones that keep him sane."

We laughed as she continued talking. I looked at her mouth as she continued to speak. "Alex told me this morning that he can't wait until you're pregnant."

There was so much happiness in the house that even if my smile turned into a frown, no one would have noticed. I looked at my stomach and grimaced at the thought.

"When you get pregnant? I don't want a baby, I'm fat enough as it is." Just then, Alex walked in and declared that we were ready to go. The combined statements sent me into temporary shock as I kissed and hugged the well-wishers goodbye. The realization of not wanting to go home and not wanting to become pregnant was definitely a strange reality.

One Year Too Long

Alex wrapped his arm around me as we walked to the car. The stiffness in my limbs riddled him with curiosity as he stopped to stare at me at the end of the walkway.

"What's wrong, you feel like a robot."

"Nothing," I replied.

The answer was too quick for him to leave me alone.

"C'mon Shanelle, I think I know you better than that by now."

He opened the door as I got into the car. The seatbelt wouldn't give way for me to lock it into place. Frustration settled into my hands as I pulled on the strap in a long jerking motion. *"See how fat you're getting, you can't even get the seatbelt on in a two seater."*

Alex quickly reached over me and loosened the strap. "Shanelle, what's wrong?" He said.

I pushed his hands away as tears began to fall. I wiped them away in swift motions and yelled, "Everything is wrong Alex! I'm frustrated and I don't know what to say or do about it."

Alex started up the car and drove down the street. Once we were out of eyesight, he pulled over. Alex put the car in park and said, "Shanelle, just say what's on your mind, start anywhere, I don't care."

I buried my head in his chest as he turned towards me. In a muffled tone I sobbed out loud, "I'm fat and I hate myself!"

Alex grabbed the back of my head and stroked my hair.

"Girl, girl, girl, there is not an ounce of fat on your beautiful body. Why are you doing this to yourself Shanelle?"

Tears kept falling uncontrollably. I wondered how long he was going to put up with me and my crying.

"I feel fat and I'm not even pregnant." Alex grabbed my face and looked me in the eyes.

"Well I don't think you're fat. Don't get me wrong, you are thick, but that's what I liked about you from the very first day I saw you. But girl, I'm not leaving you fat, thick or skinny."

My breathing began to slow down as I stared at him. The voices gathered in a huddle and attacked me.

"Quick that fucking crying Shanelle!"

" Dang, she ain't nothin' but a bitch ass crybaby."

" Girl, you better get to the real problem before he finds out."

I squeezed my eyes to shut them out. Alex kissed my forehead and said, "It's getting late, let's get on the Parkway and take care of business."

Alex headed up Parkway North and turned on CD 101.9 to calm our nerves. He sang to me during a Stevie melody as I looked out the dark windows. When we crossed the bridge, Alex pulled on my earlobe and tried to stir up small talk, but there was little he could do to engage me in conversation. Songs played that enhanced his sentiment like Patti and Luther, but there was no way Alex could begin to process my anxiety. By the time we reached Roselle, I finally decided to prepare him for Crescent Avenue.

"Alex can you turn the music down, I need to say something."

Alex obliged and shifted his hands on the steering wheel.

"What is it baby girl?"

My eyes remained focused on the white lines

dividing the traffic lanes. Twenty lines must have passed my sight until I was able to speak.

"I don't know what to expect when I get home, but my brother is not well."

Alex slowed down to pay the Union toll. He hesitated before he pulled off to look at me and said, "Shanelle, I could figure out that something wasn't right with him when he told me you were dead."

I knew Alex was an astute police officer, but I wasn't sure how much he could figure out on his own. I shrugged my shoulders and said, "Well, I think my brother wants that to happen and that's why I left home last summer. Hopefully he won't be there when we get to the house. He's been in and out of the hospital and even though it's been a year, I can't imagine that Steven got any better."

Alex sighed this time as we passed exit 144 and said, "Shanelle, I've seen so much out there in my short time as a cop, nothing seems to surprise me anymore."

I finally looked at him, hoping that he could be considerate of my past.

"I know Alex, I just didn't want to keep any secrets from you about my family."

Alex got into the right lane to exit 145 and said, "Baby, you're not the only one with secrets in your family. We all have secrets, good, bad and indifferent."

If his intentions were to dismiss the conversation, he did it by turning the radio back on to the jazz station. He pinched my earlobe and said, "We're going to be ok, trust me."

We finally turned the corner to Crescent Avenue. To my surprise, the block looked the same, but the house looked weary. The grass was unkempt and a few shingles were missing from the roof. Amazingly, Sinbad was romping around in the back and came to the gate at full attention with his ears standing straight up. When I stepped out of the car, he began to wag his tail and dropped his ears. I pointed him out to Alex and said, "He remembered me Alex, that's our dog Sinbad."

Alex put his arm around me as he stared at the exterior of the house.

"How old?" Alex asked.

"He'll be two pretty soon, I can't believe how big he got."

Alex pulled me closer to him as we walked up the pathway.

"Time flies Shanelle, that's why you've got to make the best of things while you're on this earth."

I barely processed what he said as we stepped up to the door. There was complete darkness with the exception of a flickering hallway light. I peeked through the small windowpane to see if there was anyone standing there, but it was too dark. I could hear music in the distance, but it wasn't loud enough to make out the location or direction. I put the key in the door as Alex cleared his throat and stood up straight. To my surprise, the lock had not been changed. My own wonderment immediately concluded that Steven had taken over. The lingering stench was the sign of his demise. The house smelled old and stuffy. All the windows were probably sealed shut and my first reaction was to open a window so I could breathe. I wanted to close my eyes as I walked through the vestibule. Alex held my hand as he cleared his throat again and followed behind. He closed the door as I walked to the hallway light switch. My own sense told me that the only person in the house was Steven because the house was too still. Alex reached up and tightened the tiny bulb. He pulled a tissue out of his pocket and wiped away the dusty residue from his fingertips. I stared at him for a minute, embarrassed by the uncleanly condition of the house. As soon as the light brightened the room, I gasped for air at the sudden transformation. The mirrors that I cleaned so many times were glazed over with smudge. Signs from the attic made their way down stairs in the form of old photographs, newspaper clippings and Richard Pryor albums. I was right about Steven. His calculated attempt to gain control over the house was quite visible as I turned three hundred and sixty degrees in complete shock. I stepped back into Alex's space as footsteps descended from the third floor. I whispered to Alex, "It's Steven, he's coming."

Alex barely flinched at my response as he looked up and awaited the first sight of my brother. The attic door opened from a distance and emitted the sound of an Earth, Wind and Fire tune. My body began to tense up in terror as dear brother began to take his flight down the creaky stairs. His head was hung low, but he was alert as the day he terrorized me during the winter snowstorm. As soon as his face was visible, I knew that little had changed for the good. A lot changed for the worst. His hair was matted and uncut. He had a small beard twisted into a curl. His face was riddled with acne and his once muscular frame evaporated into one lean mass. He was hunched over like the late stages of scoliosis. Laughter was his introduction to our sadistic reunion.

"Well, well, well, look what the cat done dragged in. Looking fat as ever Shanelle, but it's always good to see my chubby little sister." Steven took position by sitting on the fourth step from the landing. It was a safe position for all of us since nothing was visible from his hands or pockets.

Steven barely looked at Alex as Alex repositioned himself next to me. Steven continued to smirk under his breath as he surveyed his long lost sister. I gathered what little confidence I had and asked, "Where's mom and dad?"

His voice became deep and lethargic, "Probably singing the Lord is my Shepard with preacher man, but let's face it Shanelle, do you really give a fuck, you've been gone so long." He wasn't finished as he sucked his teeth and stared at the last step and said, "Besides, you don't live here anymore remember?"

Before I could respond, Alex came to my rescue. He sucked his teeth in disgust but had enough dignity to bypass me and extend his hand for a formal introduction.

"What's up man, I'm Alex, Shanelle's fiancé."

Steven immediately stood up and placed his hands behind his back. His street instinct immediately kicked in. His facial expression was blank and cold as he looked at the bulb in the hallway light.

"Smells like pig in here. I don't give a shit who you are, but I'll tell you one thing, you need to get the fuck out of my house, unless you have a warrant."

I was convinced by my own internal terror that mom and dad were dead somewhere in plastic bags, but Alex didn't give me a chance to think further. Alex walked up the first two steps and extended his neck just enough to look Steven dead in the eye and said, "No warrants, no bullshit, just a friendly hello and we're leaving. As you can see, your sister is very much alive, but if you keep smokin' that shit, I'm going to be saying the opposite of you in a few months." Alex backed down the stairs as I watched Steven's expression.

By this point my hand was trembling, but I knew that we were going to be safe since Steven rightfully detected that Alex was a police officer.

Steven barely moved, but he took the time out to grimace a look of evil disgust as he smiled at me. Steven remained still as Alex turned me around by my shoulders to face the front door. I was so frightened, I thought that Alex was going to pull out his Smith and Wesson and shoot him while my back was turned. This was also one time the voices remained completely silent. Instead, Alex used his free hand to open the vestibule door and escorted me to safety. I grabbed his hand tighter to secure our exit from the house. He took one last look at Steven and said, "The life you're living is like a time bomb man, take care brother."

I could hear Steven descending the stairs as we walked down the cemented steps. His disregard for Alex was in the form of silence, but he wouldn't let us leave without a final afterthought.

"Farewell you punk ass mother fuckers." Steven continued to stand in the doorway and burned a hole right through me as he laughed. He was gaining momentum because we were out of the house and Alex was no longer a threat. I was almost free and clear from dear brother, but we were moving too slow and his mind was racing with mental strategy. I could have easily dismissed his comment halfway down the parkway, but he knew me too well. As he slowly closed the creaky door, he shouted with laughter, "Find another way Shanelle, the toothpaste and peanut butter isn't working fast ass."

I stopped dead in my tracks and stared at him in astonishment. Steven nodded his head up and down as he twirled at the knots in his hair and said, "Yeah, you heard me right bitch."

Steven's comment forced Alex to stop dead in his tracks. Alex turned around and pointed his finger at dear brother like it was the barrel of a gun and said, "Yo kid, we'll meet again and trust me, the word 'bitch,' will be the last word you'll be able to say."

Steven's response was his usual psychotic routine. He stuck his middle finger up and pressed his face into the small windowpane. His eyes were wide and crazy. Rehabilitation had no effect on him as he stared at me with sheer hatred in his eyes. All the money mom and dad spent was useless. I bowed my head in defeat as I thought about Steven's verbal revelation. *Oh God, not one, but two vices exposed, how could you dear brother?"*

Alex jumped into the front seat, slammed his door and started up the car. I was frozen in time wondering what would happen next. As soon as Alex sped down the street, he started his own tirade.

"I think it's a little more than being fat don't you think Shanelle?" There was little pity in his voice. I looked at my feet in shame and then found small bits of courage to face him. I asked an innocent question with a mouth full of anxious spit.

"What do you mean?"

Alex shifted the gears back to first at the red light and said, "Shanelle, your brother was high as a hell back there, not to mention that he's not operating with a full deck."

I agreed with him and said, "I know, I told you he was sick."

Alex looked at me as if to say, "No shit Sherlock."

I looked away from him as he pulled off at the green light.

"How much of that shit did you have to put up with?"

Before I could answer, I looked at him with complete surprise. It was the first time he cursed around me. The look on my face brought him into his own realization. He quickly apologized as he touched my thigh. "I'm sorry Shanelle, I didn't mean to curse at you like that, I'm just pissed off."

His apology meant nothing to me as anger began to boil inside of me. I lashed out at him for putting me in this awful predicament. "Don't ever curse at me again!" I didn't do anything to you to deserve this. I didn't want to go and I warned you about him! What do you want from me Alex?"

The voices rallied behind me with bats and billy clubs as I quickly looked outside the window. Whatever they were saying did little to squash my frustration. Alex sucked his teeth and then laughed at my behavior. I wondered if he saw too much of my mini time bomb. He pulled into the parking lot of North Orange Park and put the emergency brake on. The force of his hand pulling the break up forced me to pay attention. I was annoyed that he stopped at the park and asked, "Why can't we just go home?"

Alex unbuttoned his shirt collar and turned the car off. He was sweating profusely as an enlarged vein surfaced on the side of his neck. I immediately looked around at the scenery. Even though the park was well lit at night, I had no interest in being there. I wanted to go home and close the blinds. My palms were itchy and my face felt extremely hot. Alex got out the car and started walking towards a park bench. He turned around, looked at me and said, "I need to think."

Worry began to consume me as I watched him put his hands in his pocket and look up to the sky. I didn't know if he was going call it quits or start hitting an innocent tree. He turned around and looked at me as I continued to hunch down. Alex motioned to me to come to him, but I refused. Instead, I slid down in my seat and crossed my arms as he sat down on a bench. Alex leaned forward and put his head in his hands. He looked defeated and tired. In retrospect, his mother was right about Alex and his determination. This was one time that he seemed stuck between a rock and a hard place. Steven had that affect on people; mom, dad and now Alex.

Tears began to swell in my eyes as I began to contemplate Alex's plot to get rid of me like rotten garbage. For once, instead of crying, my defenses festered up old habits. I forced my face into a serious expression and began looking in my pocketbook for spare change. Two tears immediately fell, but that was all that I would allow. I looked in the direction of the bus stop to see if the Forty-four bus was approaching. I could start all over again and make a clean break without judgment. New Jersey Transit was the easiest way out before I let Alex dump me.

I was so distracted in my need to find an escape that the sound of Alex opening the passenger door caught me off guard. My pocket book dropped to the ground as all of its contents spilled out. I immediately stepped out and started picking up the silver pieces. I made sure to count the fare in my head as Alex stood over me watching my every move.

In my defense, Alex bent down beside me and said, "Baby girl, forget about the change, you can't even see."

My money went directly into my pockets while I quickly shoved my makeup into the smaller compartments. I sensed eviction as beads of sweat formed on the back of my neck. The feeling was so intense I started having a conversation with one of the voices, but without realizing it, I spoke out loud.

"I need to get out of here now. The bus will be here any minute." My hands were trembling so bad that Alex had to grab them to control my movements. His face was filled with concern and worry, but he was calm in his response as he picked me up by my elbows. He searched my eyes for rationale and said, "Shanelle, stop talking crazy girl, you're not going anywhere." Alex dragged me like a rag doll to the park bench as I looked back for more coins. He gently sat me down and put his foot on the bench.

"Shanelle, you don't have to run anymore, you're safe with me. I'm not going to hurt you or leave you." He took his foot down and knelt down in front of me. "I can't imagine life without you girl despite what you've gone through. You had enough courage to leave, so give yourself credit for that." Alex grabbed my chin and stared at me. "You're brother's got a bad habit and beat your head up in the process. Things seem to make sense to me now, but I need you to open up to me so I can help you." Alex stood up and pulled me up into his arms as my body slumped into a lifeless state. He held his lips next to my ear and whispered a message of empathy. "Girl, every family has secrets locked up in little corners, behind stairs and hiding in closets. I'm going to help you get all of that garbage out of your head if it kills me." Alex's baby soft stubble brushed my cheek as he rested his cheek on the other side of my face. "C'mon Shanelle, don't do this to me, I love you girl, just squeeze me back and let me know you're with me."

Holding him brought a small sense of comfort, but I wasn't ready for anything else. I squeezed back as he rocked me back and forth as I buried my head in his chest. Weary tears absorbed into his dress shirt as he continued to hold me. I looked in the direction of the bus stop and abandoned the thought of catching an old habit. Exhaustion began to set in as thoughts of climbing into bed became me. Alex stroked the back of my head and said, "I won't ask you to do that ever again. I'm sorry your parents weren't home, but I am worried about them. I'll make a few calls tomorrow and see if I can contact your father. That way, you'll know they're safe. Our news can wait."

I couldn't find the words to speak. I was curious about Alex's need to talk to my father, but I was too tired to care. As we walked back to the car Alex said, "The only thing that prevented me from killing your brother was my love for you Shanelle and I'm not going to lose you over his addiction."

My eyes opened wide despite the emotional weights resting on my eyelids. The darkness around us compliment-ed Alex's evil intention as I looked up at him. His massive hands were enough to take the life out of anyone if he wanted to, but there was too much calm in him to think he could possibly kill someone. A chill in the air forced me to slide my hands around his waist. He hugged me back and breathed a sigh of relief in my neck.

"Ahh, that's better." He looked me in the eyes and started smiling as he said, "Now, I know you're not going to run for that bus once I let you go, right?"

A small giggle escaped from my stomach. Alex kissed my forehead and said, "You know I'm a skilled running back and I'll catch you anyway right?"

I nodded yes as he kissed me on my lips and said, "Ok then, let's go home baby girl and get those fragile wings fixed."

Alex went to the trunk and took out a blanket. He wrapped me up as I slowly put the seat belt on in silence. I closed my eyes as he started up the car and pulled out the park. The bus stop was no longer a place of surrender. Solace became me as it grew smaller through the side view mirror. As we headed down Tremont Avenue, my body rocked back and forth from small cracks and bumps on the dark winding road. I turned my head and looked at Alex for a brief second as a storm cloud took up permanent residence over my head. Steven always had a way of messing things up for me. Alex had a sharp mind and keen strategies of his own. The "fat" thing couldn't be an excuse anymore and it was only a matter of time before he began his inquiry. Just as I suspected, the third challenge was daunting, but with Alex by my side, I knew that I was going to be "somewhat" all right. Mentally drained and wounded, I drifted off to sleep with the caress of Alex's hand intermittently stroking my face. Kindness came to me in my thoughts. *"Rest now Shanelle, you're going to be okay."*

Unsettled Sheets

By the time we got home, Alex and I were exhausted. The only thing left to do was to go to bed. Alex immediately took off his clothes and took a shower. I checked on him one time and asked him if he wanted something to eat or drink, but he quietly told me "no" as I hurried out the bathroom. I closed the door to give him some privacy. My need to take a shower ran rampant in my mind. My skin felt scaly and itchy inside and out. I wanted to wash away my sins without shame and embarrassment. I pulled out some pajamas and sat quietly on the bed while Alex toweled off. My right leg shook nervously up and down in a quick and jittery response. When he came out the bathroom, I sat up at attention wondering if he was going to say anything to me, but he remained quiet. When I got up to go to the bathroom, Alex said in a deep tone, "Make sure we pick up some toothpaste tomorrow Shanelle."

I turned around and faced him but his face was tired and empty. Even if he was trying to figure me out, tonight was not the night. I grabbed some panties from the drawer but Alex stopped me with his hand and said, "Put them back."

I snatched them out the drawer just the same and quickly headed for the bathroom. The steam left over from Alex's shower melted my senses as I turned on the water. From a distance, I could hear Alex talking on the phone, but I was so tired, I didn't care who he was talking to, or what the conversation was about. I put my shower cap on and stepped inside. The water felt good against my skin as I began to apply soap to my washcloth. In order to rid myself of the entire day, I scrubbed myself twice. By the time I got out the shower, Alex was leaning on the edge of the sink watching me. The look in his eyes offered no direction or purpose. He handed me a towel as I stepped out. A warm embrace followed as he began to towel me off. Soft kisses ensued on my neck in three different places. New arousals formed inside of me even though I was ready for restful sleep. He was right; I didn't need any panties because he picked me up and carried me straight to the bed. Showers had opposite affects on us. It always woke Alex up and made me relaxed and sleepy. Alex slid beside me and stroked my damp nipples. He slid down to Kitty and swept me unconscious with his tongue. Tears engulfed my eyes as he held my hand tight upon release. Alex got up and went into the bathroom as I lay there wonderfully wounded by his love. As he gargled, I squeezed my legs tight to maintain the last ripples of pleasure as my body relaxed. Alex climbed back into bed and said, "Are you sleepy Shanelle?"

I responded by quietly whispering, "Yes."

Alex pulled the sheets up to my chin and stroked the base of neck. "Do you love me Shanelle?" Alex asked.

"Yes," I said, as I turned my body into his cinnamon frame. The vibration of the sheets between us felt soft and poetic as Alex whispered to me, "Can I make love to you right now?"

There was no way I was going to say no even though I was lifeless. I grabbed his face and pulled my lips up to his mouth. One kiss confirmed his question. I don't know what got into him, but he was definitely in the mood. He got up and pulled out one of his homemade tapes. I knew then that it was going to be a long night no matter the fatigue. His choices of songs were Minnie, Stevie, Teena and Donnie. Alex laid on top of me and slipped his tongue in my mouth as Portuguese Love serenaded his entry. I gripped my nails into his back to surrender the pain of my swollen region. My entire body melted as he entered me. Three tears rippled down my face and splashed into the cotton fabric, quickly dissolving away. The sensation of him inside of me forced my back to arch and call his name. Alex responded by burying his head in my neck and scooped his hands under my behind for extreme pleasure.

"Tell me it's all mine baby."

Soft and assured I replied, "It's yours, all of it." I squeezed him tight and wrapped my legs around his waist in pure ecstasy. Beads of sweat formed on his neck and back as he rocked and cradled me in his arms. He asked me to call his name and I whispered it over and over again until he surrendered. He pulled me on top of him and stared at me with a loving smile. I was so filled with his love I started to kiss him and intermittently call his name. As he grabbed my head I said, "Don't ever leave me Alex, I need you no matter what."

Alex squeezed me tight and settled my senses. "I told you girl, I let you go once and I'm never leaving you again."

The last thing I remembered was Alex wrapping us up in our crumpled yellow sheet and falling fast asleep in his arms.

Deadly Arrangements

To my surprise, when I woke up, Alex was in the kitchen huddled into the earpiece of the phone. He was officially on vacation and making flight arrangements with a travel agent. He called me from the kitchen and said, "Shanelle, do you have a passport?"

I yelled back, "No, I don't!" When I walked into the kitchen, he covered the mouthpiece and said, "it's okay baby, get dressed, you don't need a passport, only a driver's license and your birth certificate." I breathed a sigh of relief and went into the bathroom. I felt bad that we ran out of toothpaste, but I was resourceful. I cut the tube open and wiped the residue from the corners, making sure to leave some for Alex. By the time I got of the shower, Alex was dressed and shuffling around the apartment looking for papers and receipts. From the looks of things, he was pulling out financial statements, life insurance policies and his pension plan. He called me once he took everything out and said, "We're leaving two weeks from Sunday, so make a list of the things you need for the trip. We also need to take care of some business at the bank and the clerk's office."

I stood over Alex surveying his financial records and statements. At a quick glance, he must have come into some money because there was no way a rookie's salary afforded him that much income. Alex sat me on his lap as I rubbed the back of his head. He lost focus for a moment and started yawning. I thought the drive home and our interlude wore him out, but to my surprise, he was still worrying about me.

Alex rubbed my stomach and said, "How are you feeling today?"

There was slight hesitation in my smile, but I was able to answer truthfully.

"I'm better now that we're home." Alex rubbed the side of my leg and said, "Yeah, I like the sound of that too."

There was a look of weariness in Alex's eyes that suggested he was a million miles away. I didn't want to bring up my problems, but I had to ask out of sheer curiosity. I grabbed his chin to get his attention and said, "Hey, what's wrong?"

Alex stood up as I slid off his lap. There was too much silence in the room for us to avoid each other, so I sat down on the couch and extended my hand to him. Alex sat down next to me and laid his head in my lap like a little boy. He was deep in thought as he rubbed my legs up and down. Whatever was bothering him seemed to be buried in his chest as he began to breathe heavily. He turned over and looked at me with his head resting on my thighs. I looked into his eyes and said, "Tell me, what it is?"

He closed his eyes but no words followed. I stroked his forehead and held his other hand as he began to take slower breaths and started to yawn again.

"Sometimes people make you take on responsibilities you just can't handle Shanelle." I looked at him with a puzzled expression on my face. Alex didn't impress me as someone who had too many responsibilities that were beyond his control. I wasn't sure if he was referring to me or someone else, but I continued to support him by stroking his hairline. For a minute, I thought he was going to talk about last night, but the tone in his voice was deep and reflective. Alex continued to talk as he closed his eyes in deep thought.

"Remember that night on the beach together?" Alex asked.

"Yes baby, I remember."

"Well," Alex replied, "I told you that I only had one hurdle that would follow me until the day I die. Do you remember that?"

I nodded yes.

Alex said, "I love you enough to know that the two of us can get through anything as long as we stick together. After last night, I said to myself there is nothing that can stop us except secrets and lies."

I began to get nervous again, because I didn't know what he was trying to say. "Alex, I don't understand…"

Alex quieted me with his finger and said, "When I was thirteen, my father took us to a family reunion in Pulaski, Virginia." There was somber in his voice as he strained his face to form his words.

"I remembered how excited my sisters were to get down there and play with all of our cousins. Most of them were females and I was definitely outnumbered. We were supposed to spend four days of family time there, but like the old cliché goes, 'things fall apart.'"

Alex shifted his body and turned his head into my stomach as I stroked the outline of his ear. Watching him relax forced me into the same breathing pattern as he continued to recall his story.

"During the drive down, my father promised me he would take me fishing on the lake as soon as we settled in." He smirked at the thought and continued. "I was happy about our fishing trip. I remembered asking him at the Maryland House where the bait and tackle store was in Pulaski so we could buy some for our trip."

Alex opened his eyes and looked up at me to make sure I was listening. As I stroked his dark cinnamon skin I replied, "Go ahead, I'm listening Alex."

I was intrigued by his tale and wondered how the story was going to end. Alex sat up and said, "Funny, when we got there, it seemed like he made the whole story up just to keep my mind busy. As a matter of fact, there was one thing that he said that I won't forget."

I looked him straight in the eye and said, "What's that?"

Alex looked down at the ground and said, "He told me to look after my sisters. After that, he jumped in the front seat of my uncle's pick up truck and headed down the road."

There was no unusual meaning in what he said or what his father did, but the words that followed had rippling effects.

"Instead of looking after them, I should have kept my eyes on my mother."

Alex got up and walked into the bathroom. His head was hung low and lifeless to the ground. I wanted to help him get through his story, but I wasn't sure how I could. Luckily he continued to talk standing up.

"I remembered the look on my mother's face when he pulled off. She was so disgusted that she barely said hello to my grandmother. My hateful aunts weren't helping the situation either. My Aunt Carol came to the car and started talking junk the minute she saw her."

Alex looked around the room searching for a prop. He picked up the newspaper and rolled it up while he acted out the scene. Alex said of his Aunt, "Girl you should have known my no account brother was going to run off with Ray. You probably ain't gonna see him for a few days either, but y'all come on in this house and fetch yo'self somethin' cool to drink."

Alex seemed locked into the moment like it was yesterday.

"I can't stand my aunt Shanelle. You would think that she could have been cordial to her knowing that she felt like an outsider. That was only the second time we went to my father's side of the family for a reunion."

The look on Alex's face was filled with anger, but he continued to tell his story.

"I headed in the house with most of the bags and looked up the road for my father, but he was long gone. I damn near wanted to cry, but Willie James added his two cents in before I even got used to the idea." Alex turned up his face as he described the stranger's demeanor and said, "Boy, don't you come on this porch with that face all twisted up like that. Your daddy done all that driving and he's tired, so you best leave him alone."

Alex looked at me angry and confused. I felt like he needed me so I walked up to him and squeezed his hand to comfort him.

"Alex, let's sit down and talk, I'll make some tea." He wasn't up for the suggestion and continued to stand as he squeezed back. "You know this is hard."

"Talking about this?" I asked.

"Yeah." Alex replied.

I looked into his eyes and immediately hugged him and said. "Whatever it is, I'm here, you can tell me anything Alex."

Alex grabbed me back as he ran his fingers up the middle of my back. He seemed to be comforted by what I said and finally sat down. The kitchen was close enough not to be out of ear shot so I walked to the cabinets and pulled out his favorite mug and said, "So is Willie James, your cousin?"

Alex dropped his head in his hands and said, "Everybody called him Willie James, a second cousin from two towns over. They said he loved to drift back and forth just to eat and do odd jobs for Grandma Mae. The only talent he had was his good looks. I knew I didn't like him because he acted like he was trying to take charge in Grandma Mae's house."

I put the teakettle on and sat next to Alex because I knew he needed my complete attention.

"Shanelle," Alex said, "He was as sick as they come, eyeing up my sisters and flirting with my mother. The bastard even had the nerve to steal my sweat socks and undershirts." Alex cocked his head back just thinking about the so-called thief.

"I remembered looking for some clean socks and not being able to find any. Grandma Mae warned me, 'Boy, you better put your good stuff up because Willie James' got sticky fingers and he'll deny everything with somebody else's clothes right on his back.'"

Alex's southern impression made me laugh at first when he impersonated his grandmother. His southern drawl was highly undesirable, but he brought brevity to his anguished tale. Alex put his head in my lap again and I immediately began to massage his scalp.

"Shanelle, I was pissed off at the world that this was happening to me. My family never felt so divided and my mom never felt so alone. There was nothing I could do to please her and it seemed to me the only thing that could get her attention was that damn Willie James."

The sound of the teakettle heightened the intensity in the room. Alex jumped up and turned it off. The noise seemed to pierce his brain as he became more irritated. Alex poured the water into the teacups as he continued his story.

"I thought my father was coming back that night, but by the time we caught up with him the damage was already done." Alex looked at the teakettle and slammed it down on the stove.

"Shit," he said. "I don't want any damn tea."

There was enough worry in my mind to settle all the hot temperatures in the apartment. I quickly turned off the stove and put the cups in the sink. I walked up to him and pleaded, "Come sit down Alex."

Alex sat down in complete frustration. Then he looked at me and smiled.

"I love you so much girl, I could never stand the sight of you with anyone else." Even though his story was so compelling, I knew he was trying to open up to me like never before. I immediately kissed his lips and promised that I would never leave his side. There was so much intensity in his kiss that I thought he was going to make love to me, but he was too frustrated. Alex managed to pull himself away and finished his story.

"The next day was too much excitement for me to handle. Grandma Mae seemed to be the only person to keep a promise. We didn't have planning committees and dates for our family reunion. They just went by whatever Grandma Mae said the night before. She planned a big cat fish fry down by the river and everybody had to bring a dish. My sisters cut up sweet potatoes at Aunt Clara's house. They were happy being over there because it was a house full of women and good gossip. My mother stayed to herself at Grandma Mae's house and sulked the entire morning. She didn't want to eat and stayed to herself in Grandma Mae's room. Grandma Mae asked me to go cheer her up and see if she was coming to the fish fry."

I interrupted him and asked, "Well did you ask her if she wanted to go?"

Alex looked disappointed and said, "Yeah, I did, but when I went into the room to see if she wanted to go, she got pissed off."

Tears seemed to swell up in Alex eyes as he tried to force them back. His rugged exterior didn't allow tears, but I was glad that he felt comfortable with me.

"Take your time Alex, it's ok, I'm here."   Alex continued. "My mother told me to get the hell out of the room."

"What!" I exclaimed. "It wasn't your fault."

Alex nodded his head in agreement. "I know Shanelle, now that I think back on it, I guess she was mad at my father, but took it out on me."

I agreed with him while he continued his story.

"I knew she wanted to say those things to my father but she couldn't. I even sat on the edge of the bed to console her, but she pushed me off the bed. Grandma Mae's bed was real high, so I had to hang on to one of the posts to catch my fall." Alex scratched his head with worry. "Hmph," he said. "That bed was old and damn near ready for the junk yard, but Grandma Mae couldn't part with it. When I leaned on the post it toppled right over and landed on the floor. It was the loudest noise I ever heard Shanelle."

"Did you fix it?" I asked. The look on Alex's face diminished my anticipated answer.

"It was a temporary fix, but it came in real handy that night."

This time I laid in Alex lap hoping that he could remain calm as he finished his story. "Everybody went to the fish fry except my mother. She stayed behind with a bottle of wine and the daily newspaper. I felt sad that she didn't want to go, but I needed to watch out for my sisters, especially with Willie James around. It was so hot that day even with the lake around us. Everyone was laughing and having a good time singing songs and tellin' jokes. I tried to get into it Shanelle, but I couldn't. Every part of me felt like my mom did. I just wanted to go home.

Alex began to stroke my hairline with his hands. I was so into the story, there was no time to really appreciate his strong hands on my skin.

"Grandma Mae asked me to run up to the house to pick up some more sugar for the lemonade and you know me, I was looking for something to do and I wanted to check on my mom. I felt bad for her and I was hoping that she changed her mind about coming to the fish fry. I hopped on my cousin's bike and headed up the hill back to the house. It was hot that day too. The dust from the road kept clogging my throat. I spit a few times to clear it, but that didn't work. By the time I got back to the house, a strange silence seemed to kick in around me. Call it childhood police work, but I was curious about the surroundings of the house since everyone was down by the river. I dropped the bike by the front door and walked around the back."

Alex clenched his eyes shut like he was trying to block out a bad dream. I stroked his arm to relax him and assure him that he was safe with me. Alex looked down at me and said, "When I looked up ahead, I thought I walked in on a dead animal being devoured by a bigger animal."

Alex gripped my head with his hands as he stared at the wall. I had to grab his hands to slow down his massage. He looked down at me with blank eyes and said, "My mother was leaned up against Grandma Mae's house tongue kissing Willie James."

My mouth gaped open in pure disbelief at Alex's story, but the look on his face negated my doubt. Alex said, "The next step I took was on a small twig. I threw up on the ground and I damn near passed out. I don't know if it was the heat, the juice I drank, or my mother kissing Willie James. At least they stopped kissing when they saw me."

I sat up and looked Alex directly in the eyes and grabbed his face. "Are you ok Alex, you look sick right now?"

Alex immediately shook his head to quiet my worry for him and said, "Yeah, yeah, I'm fine baby, it just feels like it happened yesterday. I started to run towards the woods just to get away from them. Willie James was laughing out loud while my mother ran after me. He said, 'Ooooooohh weeee, look at that little piglet run. That's one fast youngin' you got there girl.'"

I felt so bad for the pain in Alex's face that I began to cry. He didn't see my tears as they slid down the side of my face and onto the couch. I brushed them away quickly and put my hand on his leg. "Alex, I'm so sorry you had to see that, what were you thinking?" Alex held his head in his hands again as he yelled out in frustration.

"I wanted to kill that bastard!" His lips began to tremble as he continued to ball up his fist.

"Damn Shanelle, why did my mother do that? She followed me into the woods and Willie James came behind her with his stupid country ass saying, 'Boy don't you go worrying about grown folks business, your mama was just having a little fun.'" Alex stood up and walked to the cabinet. He turned around and braced himself by leaning against the counter.

"I remember facing Willie James and punching him dead in the jaw, but he didn't even flinch Shanelle." The tone in his voice changed considerably. I should have admitted to Alex that watching him walk away settled my nerves as I followed his massive frame. Alex looked out the kitchen window and said, "I was surprised my mother could run so fast. She caught up to me and grabbed me like she never wanted to let go. Instead of hugging her, I pushed her to the ground. Willie James caught up to us and started laughing like a hyena. He looked at me and said, 'You little sissy, you ain't got no business pushin' yo mama like that boy.'"

Alex closed the blinds and turned to face me as I sat up. His eyes were pierced with anger as he finished his story. "I walked up to him and clocked him right in the jaw again, but he acted like it didn't faze him."

I crossed my legs on the couch and folded my arms. The intensity in Alex's voice was daunting as I asked, "What did he do next?" Alex replied, "He picked one of his big ass bucked teeth off the ground and spit." Alex started laughing as if he had a clear picture in his head. "My mother jumped up and said, 'Don't you talk to my son like that Willie, he was only trying to stop me from doing something stupid.'"

The look on Alex's face suggested that the damage had already been done. "Willie James walked off in a huff and we went back to Grandma Mae's house. I felt bad because she sprained her ankle from the fall. All she could do was apologize over and over. Part of me wanted to forgive her and part of me wanted to run away as far as I could to get away from her." Alex sucked his teeth and walked away from his own conversation as he headed for the bathroom. I watched him walk as he took his tee shirt off revealing his muscles. "Take a shower with me angel, I need you right now."

Alex's command was my unconscious will. I left the unfinished story on the couch and took off my clothes. As soon as I stepped in the shower, Alex's hands were all over my body with precision and lust. I lulled him into a quiet calm by turning up the water. Alex pulled me into his body and locked me down with a kiss. Whatever stress he had began to leave his body as he whispered my name. "Shanelle, I need you so much girl."

I put my hands through his arms and held him tight. Pellets of water bounced off his shoulders as I looked up at him. Alex wrapped his arms around me and said, "I killed him Shanelle." My heartbeat began to speed up as I looked at him in shock and said, "Killed who?"

Alex grabbed my hands and said, "Willie James, I killed Willie James." Alex began to tremble as I held his face and pleaded with him to tell me what happened. Even if the words were worth repeating, Alex couldn't bring himself to tell me what happened. He finished showering off in silence as I stepped back to give him some space. I felt lost, scared and helpless. Space was probably the best approach as he stepped out of the shower. Alex wrapped himself in his towel and put a hand towel over his head. He closed the toilet seat and sat down in perpetual shame. He wouldn't look up as he slowly turned his left foot and began to pat the floor to work his way through his story.

"The fish fry lasted until the early morning. Most of the adults were so drunk, people were saying and doing things that didn't make sense. Grandma Mae fell asleep rockin' on the front porch well into the morning and I stayed in the front room just to give my mother some space."

I began to dry off and spread lotion on my legs and arms as Alex walked into the bedroom. I followed and watched him change into some sweats. He handed me one of his tee shirts and continued his story as we sat on the bed.

"I remembered falling asleep, but not long enough to fall into a deep sleep. There was movement in the house and a draft coming from one of the windows." Alex folded his hands as he struggled to get through the story.

"You know how you think you hear something when you're sleeping but you can't figure out if you're awake or dreaming?"

I knew exactly what he meant and said, "Yeah, that happens to me all the time."

Alex replied, "I laid in bed for a while and decided to get up to see if my father finally came back. I thought it was him at first because I heard arguing coming from Grandma Mae's room. I walked up to the door and noticed a man, but it wasn't my father, it was Willie James."

Alex's story left my mouth gaping open as he said, "He was on top of my mother with his hands covering her mouth." There was a long pause and then Alex said, "That son of a bitch tried to rape my mother Shanelle."

His story seemed unimaginable but I knew he wasn't making it up. Alex had his eyes shut tight as he continued to visualize his ordeal. "I ran into the room and grabbed the knob off of Grandma Mae's bed and busted his head wide open."

I immediately covered my mouth in sheer horror as Alex stared at the floor with a blank look on his face.

"Alex, I'm so sorry," I said, as I grabbed his hand.

Alex finally looked up at me and said, "There was blood everywhere Shanelle. My mother was screaming so loud I thought she was going to wake up the whole town."

"What did you do?" I asked.

"We didn't do anything. My mother kept screaming until Grandma Mae came in the room with a broomstick ready to beat somebody. She looked at the room and said, 'What in the hell happened here?' We stood there in shock looking at Willie James like he was a freak show. It didn't take long for Grandma to gather her senses. She said, 'I aint' gonna make no judgments on you girl, but whatever happened, blood is on my grandbaby's hands.'" Alex looked down at his large hands and said, "She was right Shanelle, blood was all over me like splattered red paint."

I was so frightened by his tale that I covered my mouth to bury my own screams. Alex quickly settled me down by squeezing me tight. He rested his lips against my mouth and said, "Shh, Shh, girl, I told you I had some hurdles, you do too, but we're gonna be okay, don't worry."

I had to worry, the whole thing sounded crazy as I began to ask a million questions.

"What happened, did you go to jail, what about your mother…" I could barely finish my sentence as Alex covered my mouth again and whispered softly, "Nobody knows but us."

My eyes shifted back and forth as I became more confused. "What do you mean just us?"

Alex replied, "It didn't take Grandma Mae more than a minute to declare herself the judge and jury for Pulaski. She made us wrap him up in three of her heaviest quilted blankets and two extension cords. Before we covered his face she did the craziest thing."

"What was that?" I asked.

"She spit in his mouth and pulled a lock of her hair out. After that she put it in Willie James' hands. I don't why she did it but she did." Alex paused briefly to collect his thoughts and said, "She told us that we had to bury our secret in the darkness of the night. The sun was coming up in an hour so she made us carry his body to the pick up truck. We drove a few acres onto her property and buried him in Grandma's animal cemetery."

My mouth was wide open with disbelief as multiple images raced through my mind. "No one ever asked for him Alex?"

Alex nodded and said, "Shanelle, nobody cared. My grandmother said he was a wasted, raggedy ass no account man. He brought so much shame on the family, I think Grandma Mae was glad to see him go. It didn't matter to me though Shanelle. As numb as I felt, all I could think about was the spectacular sunrise at dawn from the back of the pick up truck."

Alex's admiration for the sunrise puzzled me as my stomach began to churn. I didn't know what he meant, but I was too exhausted to ask any more questions. Alex laid back on the bed and pulled me onto his chest.

"We went back to the house and cleaned Grandma's room from top to bottom. It wasn't until I dumped the last pail of bloody water down the drain that my father walked through the door with a stupid grin on his drunken face. My father looked at all of us and said, 'Well what the hell happened to y'all, did you slaughter a pig this morning?" The look on Alex's face was sheer disgust as he described his mother's pain. "My mother walked up to my father and started slapping and scratching him any place she could find bare skin. I wanted to jump in too, but all I could see was dried dirt and blood buried in my fingernails."

The realization of Grandma Mae's well-intentioned secret came into focus as I mustered up the energy to ask one more question. "Alex," I asked, "What about the body?"

Alex held his head up and said, "It's right there were we left it, in the animal cemetery Shanelle. No one knows but my father, mother, Grandma Mae, me and now you."

My body stiffened as if I had been inducted into a deadly cult of sin and abysmal secrets. I laid next to Alex in silence, as I stroked the soft hairs on his sculpted chest. His breathing rhythm was slow and steady. I could not get up if I wanted to. The rise and fall of his touch was my cue to be still as he slid his hand up my arm and around my shoulders. He used the tips of his fingers to stroke my skin as he said, "Shanelle, promise me you'll never leave me."

There were no pleasurable goose bumps from his touch as he applied pressure into my flesh for an answer.

I answered, "I love you Alex and I'll never leave you no matter what."

Oddly enough, Alex laughed confidently and said, "I know you won't baby, that's why I'm gonna make you my wife and the mother of my children. I felt like God gave me a second chance when I saw you at the wedding. Up until then, I was trying to atone for my sins until God gave me a sign that it was going to be alright. That sign was you Shanelle."

I snuggled into his neck as his words melted my soul. Nothing mattered with Alex, even things that were beyond his control. Alex squeezed my hand and said, "Girl, having you in my life is like sweet redemption." I closed my eyes and melted into his embrace. I wanted to fall asleep as the clock beeped to announce the noon hour. Alex shifted his head down into mine as we lay in the warmth of the afternoon sun and asked, "Is there anything about us that you want to change Shanelle?"

I wasn't sure what my answer should be as I buried his secret next to my suppressed memories. I looked into his eyes and replied, "I don't know what you mean Alex."

Alex said, "I had to tell you about my life so you could really understand how much you mean to me. After I went to your house I felt bad because I didn't want to bog you down after all the stuff you've gone through. You deserve your own downtime if you need it Shanelle."

My focus shifted to my stomach. Every one seemed to have a claim on its shape and the progress going on inside. I wanted to answer him immediately and say, *"Please, spare me with the baby stuff,"* but that was too risky. His words began to make me queasy as he continued. "Shanelle, so far I've lead this entire relationship including getting married, but I want you to let me know if it's too much for you to handle." Alex's reflective response brought tears to my eyes as I squeezed him tight and told him the honest truth.

"I want to be everything you need me to be Alex, but I'm not ready to give you a son." Even though I finished the sentence, I restricted my movement, expecting Alex to reject me on the spot. Instead, Alex began to stroke the back of my head and said, "That's a rough one Shanelle, but I understand after what happened yesterday. I promise not to put too many demands on my delicate butterfly."

I wondered what forced him to change his mind so quickly about wanting to have a baby. But the thing I worried about the most came to the surface as Alex began to break down my emotional barriers.

"I didn't forget what your brother said about the peanut butter."

I was ready to run as soon as he said it, but I only made it to the edge of the bed. Alex grabbed my arm and said, "C'mon now Shanelle, I'm not here to judge you, but don't lie to me girl. Toothpaste, peanut butter, I have sisters too and I've learned plenty watching them over the years. I'll help you get through this, but I'll tell you one thing; you need to work that out before you get pregnant even though we're going to put it on the back burner."

Tears formed in my eyes so fast there was no way I could hide them. Alex sat next to me and handed me a Kleenex from the box on the nightstand. I realized then that his mind was in constant thought and reaction to everything I said and did with him. The one thing that could get by him was the voices in my head, but for how long was anyone's guess. That was the last thing I remembered him saying as the warmth of the afternoon rested my weary eyes. My deep settling sleep was enhanced with the notion of putting motherhood on hold. Little did I know my body was engineering a different design. The reality of making love to Alex on that warm 4th of July day without a condom began to take flight. As we lay in each other's arms, deep inside the core of my womanhood, an embryo was fashioned from a fertilized egg. My innate need to sleep fostered the early signs of life that Alex so desperately craved.

Splendor in Paradise

Just as Alex planned, on the third week of our vacation, we boarded a non-stop Continental Airlines flight to Nassau, Bahamas. There was very little conversation because I was overcome with dumfounded sleep the entire flight. Alex shook my shoulders to witness the spectacular view of the crystal clear water as we landed at the Bahamas International Airport. The only thing that consumed my thoughts was a good meal and my tight pants. My stomach was so bloated that I had to unbutton my pants just to relieve the pressure. I wrapped my sweater around my waste to conceal my bloated tummy. I blamed the whole thing on humidity as Alex admired my frame and said, "Yeah, you filled out a little, but I like the look."

I was too tired to think about how I looked as we walked down the jet way. I looked up at Alex with complete jealousy. He always looked picture perfect on the worst day and was as handsome as ever. I tried to fix my clothes but abandoned the idea as we began to hear the sound of steel drums greeting us at customs. There were a few slinky girl wonders behind me giggling and chatting about their soon to be exploits on the island. One girl accidentally bumped into Alex, but after seeing the look on her face, I knew it was a flirtatious gesture. They all looked me up and down from head to toe as I pulled and tugged at my disheveled clothes. Alex laughed them off as he put his arms around me. There wasn't much hope for me as I looked down at my stomach. If Candy and I were together, I would have been more confident. Not even the sight of my handsome Alex changed my self-image. I felt fat and out of shape. Disgust overcame me as I contemplated the black one piece in my luggage. Alex grabbed my hand as we hailed a taxi. It was the strength I needed because all I wanted to do was sleep.

Alex acted like he was a native Bahamian as he chatted with the driver. We stopped at a fruit stand as Alex jumped out to stock up before we got to the villas. As Alex paid the woman, the driver said to me, "Chile, you in the Bahamas man, there's no time for sleepin' less you got baby." I sat up quickly and said, "No sir, not yet, we're getting married." The driver smiled through the rear view mirror as if he had a secret. He put the car in park and said, "If you say so."

Alex didn't' entertain our conversation as he bit into an apple. He leaned into me and asked, "Do you want a bite?" I shook my head no as the driver wittingly replied, "That's how Adam got in trouble man." Alex and the driver laughed in unison as my eyes rolled back in my head for a second sleep filled nap. The taxi driver took us on a small tour as I continued snoozing. The two of them laughed and joked about our upcoming nuptials on the island. He pointed out a few social spots as we headed to the West Cable Beach condominiums. Alex tipped the driver as he helped us with the bags. I apologized for being sleepy as Alex looked at me and laughed. "Are you planning on sleeping the whole trip Shanelle?"

Before I could answer, a familiar face barreled out of villa number two screaming with open arms.

"Shanelle!"

It was Candy and the minute I spotted her I ran up to her and grabbed her as we fell crashing to the ground. Alex started laughing and said, "Damn, I don't get that kind of a reception." Candy and I jumped up barely brushing the sandy residue off our clothes. "You lied," I said. "I thought you weren't coming!" Candy grabbed my cheeks and said,

"And miss your big day, I don't think so."

A tall gentleman stepped out of the villa smiling at all of us as Candy turned to introduce us. "This is Clinton everyone, that's Shanelle of course and her fiancé, Alex." The two of them gave each other dap like they knew each other from back in the day. I smiled at the both of them as I quickly caught Candy looking at my midsection. She noticed the look on my face and pinched my cheek.

"Hey," Candy said, "Let's go inside where it's cooler." I grabbed her hand to follow her, but Alex had other plans for me.

"Yeah, but let me get settled with Shanelle and we'll hook up in three hours for dinner."

Clinton nodded his head in approval as he started pulling Candy back to her villa. I waved goodbye to my girl like old times. She winked at me in return. My girl knew we would have time together later on and didn't need to say anything. She was the perfect surprise for our wedding ceremony.

Alex and I checked in at the registration desk amidst a small crowd of young couples in the lobby. There was nothing I needed to do except wait for him to take care of everything. I looked at some brochures and surveyed some of the tourist attractions. The stimulation from the entire day must have overwhelmed me because I needed to sit down. My feet and hands felt extremely heavy and I was hungry. Alex handed me the paperwork and room keys as the bellhop loaded our luggage onto the cart. By the time we got back to the room, I was ready to pass out. Alex took one look at me and said, "Shanelle, you need to eat something, you slept the entire flight remember?"

"I know, I know," I replied. "Can I order from room service?"

"Sure, you don't have to ask Shanelle, get whatever you want."

I surveyed the menu and ordered a garden salad but Alex wasn't satisfied. "Shanelle, order some food, a salad isn't going to fill you up." I was too tired to get annoyed, so I grabbed some fruit and said, "I'll be fine, I'll make up for it at dinner, I promise." I walked into the bathroom to wash my face and hands before I took a shower. Alex didn't get in with me like he usually did. Instead, he chose to lean against the sink and watch. He left for five minutes and came back with a towel and handed it to me.

"Your food is here. I added some chicken breast to your order Slim Jim."

Funny, I didn't feel slim, but I knew I had to go along with the program. Alex sat on the bed and turned on the TV while I ate at the table. I ate it so quickly I didn't realize that he was watching me.

"Feeling better?" He asked.

To be honest, I felt much better as I jumped on the bed next to him. Alex took my towel off and threw it on the floor as he replied, "I want you Shanelle."

Without hesitation I said, "I want you too, but did you bring any condoms?"

"No," he retorted. "Did you get your period yet?"

I was puzzled by his question and said, "I don't think this is about whether or not I'm getting my period, I thought we agreed."

"We did," Alex replied, "but from the looks of things, you may not get your period."

I looked at Alex like he was crazy. "Stop playing Alex, that's not funny." He pulled me closer to him and started rubbing my stomach. "I know what we said mommy, but it may be too late."

I wanted to be mad at him as I pushed him away. I got off the bed and went into the bathroom, making sure to close the door behind me. The mirror presented no clues or revelations. I looked the same, except for the swelling due to the humid temperature. My skin looked clear and my eyes didn't look so dark. I thought to myself, "He can't be right, I'll talk to Candy about it later."

Alex knocked on the bathroom door and said, "Are you okay mommy?"

"Stop calling me that Alex," I said.

He laughed and said, "Ok, babe, but I still want you."

I yawned and said, "Okay, I'm coming."

I walked out of the bathroom while Alex continued to stare at me. I looked at the silly grin on his face and said, "What?"

He laughed to himself and said, "Absolutely nothing, I love you and you're all mine."

Alex took a shower while I stretched out across the bed. Before I knew it he was peeling away at my tee shirt and panties with his teeth and hands. The places he touched were so fulfilling it didn't take long for me to respond to him the same way. He took the time to take the phone off the hook and put a hickey on my hip. I pushed his head away and said, "I need to use the bathroom." He picked his head up and said, "Make it quick, we're going to dinner at six."

I ran into the bathroom and shut the door. This time the mirror told a different story. I didn't realize how much weight I put on in the last two weeks. We never bothered to work out with all the planning to get here. My breasts and stomach looked extremely swollen. I even wondered what I was going to wear. There was no way my shorts were going to fit as I began to panic. I turned on the shower and stepped into the hot stream. I looked down at my stomach again. The size and shape of my stomach looked bigger under the water. I held my stomach in, but it offered little recourse. It swelled back out like a small balloon. I also felt full like I ate two double cheeseburgers. "Maybe it's the food," I thought. The voices had a different version and they were ready to tarnish me. *"Don't even think about crying, I think you've just made Alex a happy man."*

The shower did little to settle my nerves as I climbed into bed. The sight of Alex was unsettling too as he nuzzled next to me. As we made love, I felt unconnected. A hollow ache filled my heart from everything he said and did to me.

The realization of my thoughts came together as I said to myself, "Could I really be pregnant?" The thought overwhelmed me as Alex called my name and rocked me in his own pleasing rhythms. I called his name when he asked me to but it was only to please him. Nothing made sense to me as he released himself inside of me. "A baby?" I thought. "I don't want a baby. I don't want to be pregnant. What about school?" Alex started to kiss me long and hard as I stroked his back.

"Don't ever leave me girl."

I pulled my lips away from his and whispered in his ear. "I won't, I promise."

Alex looked at his watch and rolled over. He was sleep in an instant, as I lay there hollow and empty. I began to rub my stomach to ease my worry, but it offered little answers. Before Alex fell into a deep sleep he rolled over and pulled me into his massive frame. I was tucked into him like a little child as I held him tight, afraid of my own existence. There was nothing left to do but close my weary eyes and sleep my thoughts away.

Quiet Reflection

After making love to Alex and one full hour of sleep, I was in no condition to go out. Since the villa included a full service kitchen, I made some tea and went to the back patio. It was already 5:00 pm and the sun was settling over the Caribbean waters. A small white table and chair was my resting place as I kicked my sandals off and got settled. There was a full ocean view in front of me to reflect on my life in its entirety. Something stirred inside of me to check on Alex. After a brief peek through the curtains, it was clear that he was in no condition to go out either. I kissed his forehead and covered his shoulders with the sheet. He took comfort in my gesture of affection by smiling slightly as he rolled over. I watched him sleeping for a minute and smiled. He looked so content and safe in our little world. The trauma he experienced was far worse than mine and I imagined that our quiet existence was all he wanted. I stroked my collar bone and wondered what we would have to go through to cope despite the trauma in our lives. I wanted to put the past behind me at Crescent Avenue, but I knew that Alex's dilemma would have lifelong consequences. Now that I knew his secret, I wondered if I had the stuff to keep him settled and happy. I returned to the patio and leaned against the doorway. The beauty of the ocean and its accompanied breeze was so relaxing I was convinced that we should never leave the island. I held my face up to let the sun bask on my cheeks and forehead. It was so warm and inviting that I pulled my chair to the edge of the deck. I sat down and looked at my stomach. Little had changed as I rubbed it in small circular patterns. I thought to myself, "With classes starting in September, could I really be pregnant?" My immediate response was tainted with confusion. "I can't be, could I?" I began to think about how many times Alex made love to me without using a condom and it was clear that he had plenty of opportunity to get the job done. We only used a condom on July 4th, but after he slipped the ring on my finger, we made love again without using one. I guess in Alex's mind I was his and that was that. My mind shifted focus as I looked at the crashing waves coming on shore in a thunderous applause. The water was as daunting as my life; small waves rifling towards shore, suddenly being sucked back into a more powerful force. Powerless to the elements, small bubbles surfaced and quickly dissipated as the large swell took over. The house on Crescent Avenue claimed me mentally, had Alex done the same? I wanted a donut, maybe even peanut butter, but I knew that I couldn't do it with Alex around. I thought to myself, "Why did you make those promises?" I loved him too much not to, but did I have a choice? I took a deep breath and watched the swell of my stomach rise and fall. Suddenly a warm hand touched my shoulder. A soft kiss on my cheek followed as he knelt down next to me.

"Can't sleep?" asked Alex.

I caressed his face and said, "No, just thinking.."

Girl Talk

Alex convinced me to make a mad dash for the bathroom to get dressed for dinner. I pulled my hair back in a ponytail and grabbed a sundress from my suitcase. It was tight but bearable as he rushed me through the process.

"Hurry up Shanelle, I told them dinner at six o'clock."

"I'm coming!" I shouted. "I need to get my sandals on." Embarrassing as it was, Alex had to fasten them for me as I rested on his hips. He slid his hands up my legs and grabbed his treasure. I pushed him away and said, "Stop, is that all you can think about?" Alex backed up and said, "Let's go."

I was glad to see Candy when we got outside. She looked me up and down, hugged me again and said, "You look cute." I smiled and said, "You're gorgeous as ever." Clinton rolled his eyes in his head and said, "C'mon man, let's sit up front so they can compliment each other all night."

We boarded the minivan and took an evening tour of the island before dinner. Candy whispered in my ear and said, "What's wrong, you don't look like you're going to be married in two days?" I gave her a look as if to say, "Not now."

The driver drove to Paradise Island as Candy patted my hand. I felt trapped by the whole idea of baby and marriage. Being with Candy, as free as she was, made the realization more clear. But there was nowhere for me to go and I was in no position to say no. As we exited the vehicle,

Alex extended his hands to me and said, "Still mad?"

I looked at him and said, "No, just a little confused."

Alex put his arms around my shoulders and said, "I've got cold feet too, but we're going to work this out. No secrets right?"

Before I could answer, he started pulling me towards the beach and said, "Tell me you don't love me Shanelle. Tell me that I didn't wait a year to make love to you for the first time. Tell me that I haven't been there for you through school, your bills, your brother, the weight thing and now the food issue. Tell me now and I'll leave you alone." I quickly put my head down in shame. There was no way I could tell him I needed space to breathe despite it all. I looked up at him and he was still there, too good to be true and as handsome as ever. The island, along with Alex's cinnamon complexion did nothing but enhance his demeanor and love for me. I grabbed him around his waist and said, "I'm sorry."

Alex breathed a sigh of relief and said, "No need to apologize baby, let's eat and you are going to eat."

The four of us sat down to a splendid dinner filled with lobster, grouper fish, conch fritter, cabbage and rice and peas. I was in seventh heaven as I sampled Candy and Alex's plate after heartily eating my own dinner. Alex smiled at me in sheer delight while Candy watched me in dietary horror.

"Shanelle," Candy asked, "When are you going to come up for air?"

Alex started laughing and jumped into the conversation. "Leave her alone, she's hungry."

I started laughing, but Candy didn't find it funny at all.

"Let's go to the bathroom girlfriend," Candy said. She rolled her eyes at Alex and grabbed me by the wrist. As light as she was, she flung me into the bathroom with an attitude.

"So, what's up girlfriend, you lost your mind or something? Alex is damn near finishing your sentences. Even Clinton said that you're not the person I described. Who's calling the shots?" Candy was ruthless. All I could do was bust out in nervous laughter. I had to laugh because I didn't have a comeback and I usually did. But when she wouldn't stop staring at me the emotions from my past came right back and it was written all over my face.

"Girl, do you know what you're doing?" asked Candy.

"Yeah."

Candy looked me up and down and said, "I don't know whether to smack you or buy you a pregnancy test."

"I'm still going to school in September, I didn't forget my plans.

Candy shook her head and said, "You shouldn't forget your plans but everything in your life is happening so fast Shanelle and most of those decisions are being made by Alex."

One tear spilled from my face as she wiped it away.

"Loving Alex is a good thing, but don't let him dictate everything Shanelle."

"You're right Candy," I said. "Let's go back to the table."

When we returned, Alex and Clinton were laughing and joking about sports. They both stood up to assist us back into our seats.

"Anyone care for dessert?" Alex asked.

We all responded in unison, "No!" The spontaneous comment brought brevity to the room as Alex stood up and asked me to dance. I took his hands as he led me to the small dance floor."

Alex whispered in my ear, "In one day lady, you and me, man and wife, how does that sound?"

I looked up at him and said, "Sounds wonderful."

He replied, "Are you sure you don't mind waking up to this face every morning?"

I laughed and said, "Nope, don't mind at all."

Alex held my hand up, looked at my engagement ring and said, "That means a lot to me Shanelle, you're my lady now and forever."

I rested my head on his chest as the Caribbean rhythms swayed our bodies to and fro. Clinton and Candy held their glasses up to us as Alex smiled at them. The music, food and warmth of Alex's embrace was all the comfort I needed.

Wedding Day

The sun rose on our wedding day without hesitation. I woke up to the sound of the phone ringing. It was Candy whispering in the earpiece. "Shanelle, come to my villa, Clinton went for a jog and I need to see you."

I turned and looked at Alex. He was fast asleep and it looked like he needed to get an extra hour of sleep. In lightening speed, I threw on one of Alex's tee shirts and ran to Villa number two. When I opened the door, Candy was standing there with a box in her hand. She turned it over in the palm of my hand and said, "Pee on it, you just woke up and it'll be real accurate."

"EPT?" I ask.

"Yeah, an early pregnancy test. Take it, you owe it to yourself."

At her command, we walked into the bathroom. Candy opened the package and said, "Don't fuck this one up, this damn thing cost forty bucks in the Bahamas."

The cost factor meant little to me as I put the stick into the stream. Candy took some toilet tissue off the roll and sat it on the counter top and said, "Here, put it on the tissue."

As the toilet began to flush, we watched the liquid spread across the two lines and almost immediately, two purple lines popped up. Candy's face went from curious to shock.

"What?" I asked.

"Two purple lines Shanelle, that means you're pregnant."

I grabbed the stick and said, "Let me see that box." Just as I began to read the instructions, there was a knock at the door.

"Shit," Candy said, "It's Alex."

I quickly wiped myself and pulled my tee shirt down as the sound of Alex's flip flops headed through the front door.

"Is Shanelle here?" Alex asked.

"Yeah, she's in the bathroom."

Alex walked in and surveyed the coral décor. He looked at me and said, "What's up, everything ok?"

"Yeah, everything is fine."

"What's that?" He asked, as he pointed to the box in my hand.

Candy stood in the doorway as I looked at the box and said, "It's a pregnancy test."

"Oh," Alex replied. He leaned up against the tile wall with the palm of his hands and said, "Well?"

"Well what? I replied.

"Did you pass the test?" He asked. His face was quite serious and I knew what answer he wanted to hear. He turned around and looked at Candy, but she shrugged her shoulders and backed off.

Alex closed the door and walked over to me as I backed into the sink. He looked down at me and grabbed my face in the palm of his hands and said, "Tell me Shanelle, you're killing me."

I held the kit up to him and said, "I'm pregnant."

Alex dropped to his knees and kissed my stomach in fifteen places. "Look at you! I knew it, I knew it, but I didn't want to say anything until I was sure. You just made me the happiest man in the world!" Alex picked me up and carried me out of Candy's villa as she watched us in slow motion. Clinton was coming in from his jog as Alex exclaimed, "Man this is my lucky day!" Clinton gave us the peace sign as he closed the door after our exit.

When we got back to our villa Alex laid me on the bed and squeezed the life out of me. "Girl, do you know how happy I am right now?"

I stroked his face and said, "Happy indeed."

Alex kissed me all over and rubbed his hands along my stomach as he sang a lullaby to his little seedling. He looked ridiculous, but I didn't say a word. I was amazed how such news gave him so much fulfillment, yet made me feel hollow and empty. When he finished, I got up, laid my white sundress out like nothing happened. Alex was in the shower singing and humming away all of his past sins and aggression. As he sang, my little island friends popped up to greet me. The Little One said, *"Barefoot, fat and pregnant."* The Big One replied, *"She's going to pack it on too, at least fifty pounds."* I laughed at the both of them and hoisted my dress in the air so it could fall flat on the bed for ironing. I said out loud, "That test was wrong, my period is coming, I can feel it."

"Did you say something Shanelle?" Alex was coming out of the bathroom and overheard my conversation.

"No, I didn't say anything."

He grabbed me from behind and pressed his hands on my stomach and said, "Today is our big day mommy."

"It sure is." I replied.

By 11:00 am we were standing before Reverend Timothy Simons. With his bible in tow, we took our vows before God, Candy, Clinton and the reverend's three children. His youngest daughter was five months old and cute as a button. I was attuned to the ceremony, but I couldn't help looking at her little hands and feet in the hot sun. She started to get fussy, so her older sister carried her in the house for a nap. The distraction gave me enough time to tune in to our nuptials.

"Do you Shanelle Brown take Alex Foster to be your lawful husband, to have and to hold till this day forward till death do you part?"

"I do," I replied. The cool wind forced some of the petals free from my gardenias sending them to the ground. Candy and I simultaneously watch them slip away and land onto the grass. I looked down at them and then looked up at Alex. He picked my chin up as Reverend Simons simultaneously said, "You may now kiss the bride."

It was as simple as that. Candy kissed me, Clinton hugged me and Alex smiled the whole time. There were no fireworks, orchestra or proud parents. The whole thing felt so surreal. I wondered if I was dreaming.

I had to say goodbye to Candy three hours after the ceremony. Clinton and Candy had to get back to Pittsburg. They didn't have the luxury of time that Alex and I had. She squeezed my hand in the back seat of the taxi and joked about our unexpected news.

"I'm not changing diapers unless it's a girl." Candy said.

Alex turned around and smiled at her as I gazed out the window. My engagement ring and delicate gold wedding band did little to ease my stigma. I remained quiet all the way to the airport as Alex occasionally looked back at me and smiled. At the airport, Alex and Clinton shook hands and exchanged business cards. Candy pulled me out of the minivan and forced a smile on my face. "I know you're going to miss me, but you'll be fine, I know you will. School will be over in October and we'll be on the move in no time." Her words did little to comfort me.

"How can I with a big ole belly?" I asked.

Candy pinched my cheek and hugged me. "Girl, you're going to be ok. Alex is a good man and he'll take care of you, just don't forget what I said. You have a voice too you know."

My eyes rested on the ground as I said, "I know, I know. But listen, don't forget Alex is leaving Monday and I'll be by myself for a whole month... call me."

Candy started walking away and said, "Okay, I won't forget."

Alex put his arms around me as we watched them walk into the terminal. He looked at me and said, "Are you ready for our honeymoon?" I looked up at him and said, "We've been honeymooning since July 4th, remember?" That devilish grin of his extended from ear to ear. He opened the door and said, "You can take us to the villa sir."

When we got back to the villa, to my surprise, Alex had the back deck decorated with white candles. Pink and white flower petals adorned the pool and a lobster dinner was waiting for our consumption.

"This is beautiful Alex, thank you." I said.

"Anything for you Shanelle, let's eat."

We sat by the poolside as Alex made a plate for me. I poured wine for him and spring water for myself. I decided to exercise some self-assertiveness and said, "Hopefully my course schedule will be there when we get home. I signed up for International Politics and a creative writing workshop, I hope I got in."

"That's good," Alex replied.

"There's also a peer leadership class with a young professor from Rutgers, they say she's really good too."

"Oh yeah?" Alex said.

I took a bite of some bread and said, "Eighteen credits is a heavy load, but I'm sure I'll manage."

Alex looked down at my feet and said, "You should put your feet up, they look swollen."

I looked down and confirmed it by shaking my head and said, "They are, but I'm fine."

Alex took a deep breath and said, "We need to find

a good obstetrician in the area, you need an appointment."

I looked down at my plate of food and suddenly, I wasn't so hungry. I looked up at him and said, "I've been cramping a lot lately, I think my period is just late Alex."

Alex took a sip of his wine and said, "Sounds like implantation to me."

"Implantation?" I asked. "What's that?"

"Oh, just our little one settling in, Mary had the same thing with my nephew."

"Oh," was my response.

Alex took another sip and said, "If it gets too much for you, you may want to drop a class or..."

I didn't let him finish his sentence. "Oh no, I'm going full steam ahead, I want to graduate in four years Alex, not five, or even six."

"Ok, ok," Alex replied. "I was only looking out for you and the baby's best interest."

I pushed my plate of food away from me and said, "I'm not hungry anymore."

Silence accompanied Alex's slow sip of wine. He put his glass down and wiped his moist lips as he continued to stare at me. Then he started to take off his shoes and socks while I watched him. He removed his tie and started unbuttoning his shirt and said, "Get in the pool with me Shanelle."

I looked at the pool. It was warm and inviting as the moon shined against the rippling water. Alex stood up and took his clothes off except for his underwear and got in the deep end. He went underwater for a minute and came up for air.

"Get in mommy," Alex said.

I sipped my water and continued to stare at him. A steel drum band was playing in the distance as he extended his hand to me. "Don't make me wait baby, come here." I started to take off my clothes, but he held up his hand and said, "No, I'll take them off."

Beads of water rolled off his handsome face as I stepped into the water. My dress bellowed up to the surface as Alex lifted it over my head. He bit into my breast as I grabbed his head. There was an intense tingling sensation that I never felt before. I enjoyed it, but it felt different. Alex began to kiss me as I held him tight. He hoisted my leg up and I obliged by wrapping my legs around his waist. He looked at me and then kissed me hard again. When our eyes met, I opened up to him and said, "I'm scared Alex. I don't know how to do all of this stuff, especially baby stuff. We were supposed to put this on the back burner remember?"

He shook his head and said, "I remember, but it happened already and there's no turning back right?"

"Right." I replied.

Alex breathed a sigh of relief and said, "Well then let's enjoy our time together. We have two days left on the island and we're going to enjoy it."

I started to yawn as I shook my head in agreement to his plans. He smiled at me and said, "You look tired, let's go to bed and start fresh tomorrow."

"Sounds like a great idea," I replied. I stepped out of the pool and wrapped a towel around my body. The weariness I felt was my body working overtime as I slipped into dry clothes. Alex went to the kitchen area and placed a call back to the states. My eyes began to close the minute my head hit the pillow, but I could hear Alex's conversation as he cleared his throat. He sounded elated the minute he began to speak.

"Hey mom. Yeah, everything's fine, it's official. Shanelle? She's resting right now and for a good reason. No, I'm not kidding, she took a pregnancy test today. No kidding, I swear ma. Yeah, that is good news. What? No, we'll be back on Monday morning. No, we have a few things to straighten out, but she'll be fine. I know, I know ma, I'll tell her tomorrow. Right... Well she can drink orange juice until she sees the doctor. Ma? Before you hang up, I want you to know that I told Shanelle..., Ma, I had to tell her. She won't judge you ma, trust me, we'll be fine. Listen, I got to go, it's my honeymoon you know. I love you too... bye."

Alex quietly returned the phone to the base and shuffled around the kitchen. The faucet released water as I tried to figure out what he was going to do next. As soon as the sound ceased, I closed my eyes in anticipation for his touch. He sat on the bed and gently smoothed out my satin gown along the side of my hip. He ran his hand down and around my stomach with the tips of his fingers. He kissed my cheek and said, "I love you Shanelle Foster." I responded by balling up into a tight fetal position.

"He really does love me," I thought, as my eyes grew more and more weary. Sure, maybe I was too tired for romance on our honeymoon, but I knew he would understand. There was simply too much information in my brain sending me into mental overload. Besides, if I was pregnant, it only supported my need to sleep.

Exhaustion overwhelmed me as my lids closed shut for the night. Sleep seemed to be my only priority.

The sound of chatty birds woke me up at 8:00 am. Alex was already up and about, sitting on the deck reading the newspaper. After a quick shower and ponytail prep, we headed out to Johnnie Canoe's for breakfast. Conch fritters, scrambled eggs and cantaloupe decorated my plate as I ate with smooth precision. I was surprised at how hungry I was as Alex beamed with pride. I didn't dare resist when he poured orange juice in my glass.

"Folic acid is the best thing for you right now mommy," Alex said.

"Are you going to call me mommy from now on?" I asked.

"Yeah, it suits you perfectly; besides, you're too cute to resist."

Slow sips preceded his comment as I stared at him through my glass. He watched me drink the whole thing and said, "I'm glad to see that you're eating Shanelle." I picked up a piece of his biscuit and said, "Me too." A brief pause followed as I looked for the bathroom sign.

"I need to use the restroom," I said. My demise was cool and calculated as I headed for the door. "Quick, wash your hands," I thought. The first stall looked spotless as I went inside. Kneeling down in a stooped position, I held onto the toilet bowl handle, put my face over the bowl and with one swift action, I shoved my pointer finger down the back of my throat forcing the creamed substance into the bowl.

"Good one Shanelle," the Little One said, "You can blame this on morning sickness too." I closed my eyes and rested the palm of my hand on my forehead. My face felt hot and flushed. A woman walked in as I exited the stall. The rush of the cold water out of the basin relieved my dizziness and brought me back to focus. I felt much better as I patted water on my face. Pulps of orange juice sat in my gums as I rinsed my mouth three times.

"Are you okay miss?" The kind woman asked.

"Yes, I'm fine, thank you." When I walked out, the Big One conjured up a cruel intention.

"Wish you could spit that thing up inside you too, huh missy?"

Shock forced me to stand still for a minute. "How could they be thinking such a horrible thing?" I shook my head as I walked back to the table.

"What's got your face all turned up?" Alex asked.

"Nothing, my stomach is just a little upset," I replied.

"Oh," Alex replied.

"Upset my ass," the Little One said.

"Are you ready Alex?"

"Sure, let's go."

We caught a taxi to the Artasda Zoo to see the famous flamingo run. It was cute, but the warm swell of the Bahamian sun beating down on us sent me into a dizzy spell. Purging was a bad move on my part as I begged Alex to take me back to the villa. He felt so bad for me he carried me by piggyback to the exit as he hailed a taxi. Once we settled in, Alex ordered some crackers to settle my stomach and put a cool compress on my head.

"We're staying in for the rest of the trip," Alex said. "I don't need you getting sick away from home."

I didn't want to be sick, pregnant or pampered. But the reality of it all was being forced upon me with little choice.

A good nap was all I needed. Alex ordered two turkey sandwiches and fresh fruit. It was a good choice because I was starving and didn't want to admit it to him.

"This looks delicious, come sit down and eat with me," I said.

Alex sat down next to me and gently put his hand on my thigh. "Is that okay?" He asked.

"What?" I replied.

"Touching you like that?"

I put my hand on his face and said, "Don't be silly, of course you can touch me there," I said.

"Funny," Alex replied, "I did that the other night and you damn near took my head off."

I pondered the statement and nodded. "Yes you're right."

Alex smiled in gest as he took a bite out of his sandwich. He slid his hand further up my thigh as I stared at him.

"Still hungry?" he asked.

"Yeah, for you," I replied. Alex finished chewing his food and said, "Well, sometimes I don't know how to read you."

"Well maybe I don't want to be read Alex." Alex removed his hand and placed both of his on his lap and said, "Well how will I know, because the other night didn't sit right with me?"

I took a sip of water and looked at him. His eyes looked serious but concerned. I replied, "Just ask."

Alex stood up and planted a kiss on my forehead. "I'm getting in the pool, oh, I'm also asking."

I looked up at him and smiled. "Ok, give me a minute, I'm coming." I thought to myself, "Mr. Foster is smooth, very smooth."

Alex left the sliding glass door open as he got into the pool and began to do laps. I wanted to finish eating and sit for a minute while he waited. A small notepad and pen was sitting on the table. I turned it around to see what Alex wrote. "Dr. Robinson, obstetrics. Well isn't he the eager beaver," I thought to myself. I tore the paper off and put it to the side. I wanted to write something to organize my thoughts. So much had happened in the last few weeks, I wondered how I would remain sane. The title came quickly as I watched Alex methodically cut the waters surface with his lean arms.

The Dance

I left a cold place a brief time ago,
an abyss of cruel intentions.
A beautiful place became me
in the warmth of cinnamon arms.
Perhaps my naivete suppressed
a tale of unspeakable wrath,
hidden among the maple trees,

down a horrendous path.

Innocence is a place I found,
wherever sorrow appears.
Tucked away in mental anguish,
Buried in a million tears.

A delicate hand rests inside his
sweet and protective touch.
Security forces surrender.
Your love means so much.

You lead, I follow,
A dance among stars.
A tiny seed grows within.
Determination my love,
how lucky you are.

Is this a paradox?
A rare treasure?
Only two should know.
Appearing so confident,
hidden emotions ebb to and fro.
The path beside me so complex,
a delicate life strengthens and grows.

The maiden sighs today,
it settles beneath her brow.
He who ponders deadly sacrifices,
hand in hand we take a bow.
She awaits...
Time...
Perpetuity...
He waits...
Seasoned...

Perhaps too secure,
My husband, now and forever more.

I signed it Shanelle Foster, the first time I ever accepted my new married identity. I left it on the table for Alex to read later and joined him in the pool. He was at the opposite end when I stepped inside. The forced temperature upon my skin made my nipples hard as goose bumps rose up my arms and legs. He said nothing, but stared. I backed up against the edge and rested my arms on the pool's edge. He looked at me with a devilish grin and went under as I watched his body swan out to my side. He held his breath under the water and took my panties off as they floated to the surface. When he reached the surface, he abruptly kissed me long and hard. The sound of the water rippling between our touch was the perfect orchestra. Alex took my bra off and put it on the edge of the pool as he bit my breasts. A sharp and pleasurable pain ripped through me as I grabbed his head. He picked me up and carried me out of the pool and onto the bed soaking wet. Alex buried his face in Kitty and rocked her into a sweet melody as I began to cry. He turned me over and kissed the small of my back and ran his hands up and down my legs as I called his name. He bit my back as he entered me and ran his hand up the nape of my neck and hair. The feeling was so intense, unlike anything I had ever felt before. We rolled over as Alex straddled me on top of him and locked us into a quiet rhythm. His face was filled with pleasure and intensity as he called my name. There was no place for us to surrender as we continued to make love along with the island breeze. We turned over again. Alex laid on top of me and entered me again. His words were soft and unforgettable. "Shanelle, you feel so good, I'll die for you girl." His words and rhythms forced tears to flow as I called his name. My body began to shiver as I released my own pleasure onto him. Soon after, Alex succumbed as he collapsed on top of me. The weight of his body was too heavy, especially on my stomach.

Alex realized his own pressure was against me and quickly rolled off. He placed his hand on my stomach and said, "I forgot, did I hurt you?" I grabbed his face and said, "No, we're fine." He smiled as he grabbed my face and said, "I like the sound of that. Do you think you're coming to terms with this?"

I wiped my forehead with the palm of my hand and said, "I don't have much of a choice do I?"

Alex immediately got off the bed and headed for the shower. I said the wrong thing, but he needed to hear it even though we just finished making love.

"Shanelle!" Alex said.

"Yes," I replied.

"Get in here."

"Excuse me?" I asked.

Silence followed. I didn't like the tone in his voice, or the way he called me. Anything that sounded like the path I used to follow needed immediate rejection. The only thing I couldn't reject was his baby. I looked at the swell of my stomach. After the orgasm I had, it seemed to swell double the size. I went to the bathroom hoping to see Aunt Flo, but she was nowhere to be found even after the pounding Alex gave me. Alex peeked through the shower curtain and said, "Shanelle, it kills me when you say things like that. Do you know how happy I am? Damn, it's like everything is going my way and…"

"That's just it Alex, everything is going your way, how about my way, or better yet, how about our way. I'm starting my sophomore year in college and you're leaving for a month, why does it seem like I'm carrying the brunt of all of this, babies, books, Dr. appointments and missing you."

"Whoa, whoa, Shanelle," Alex replied. He began

vigorously scrubbing his head and yelled over the stream of water, "The last time I checked, I was walking out the door everyday to put you through school. I'm not asking you to give that up, we need that." He emphasized "we," and looked me up and down like he could not believe what I was saying.

"Yeah, but already you're trying to break me down to nine credits and sleep exhaustion. I would have preferred to go full steam ahead without..." I couldn't finish my answer as Alex stepped out the shower and walked up on me.

"Without what Shanelle? Are you trying to tell me something even though you know how much this baby means to me?"

I sat down on the toilet defeated. "There's nothing left to say Alex."

"Damn," he said, as he grabbed me by the arms. "Look at us having our first argument on our honeymoon, girl, I don't want to do this."

"Me either," I replied.

"*You punk,*" The Little One said. I squeezed Alex tight, surprised that they were still creeping up on me like that.

"Let's order some ice cream from room service, I need something sweet," Alex said.

Room service came in five minutes flat as we ate my favorite chocolate chip mint with hot fudge. The last remnants of a honeymoon left us that night as the real world rolled in. Alex crossed his ankles and leaned against the headboard with the remote skillfully locked in his hands. I placed my bowl of ice cream on my swollen tummy and wolfed down cold spoonfuls of my favorite desert. We shared no laughter and exchanged no flirtatious glances. We left sentences unresolved. Emotional entanglement rested between us in the form of two pillows. I got up to brush my teeth while Alex hurled his first post wedding mental assault.

"Leave me some toothpaste Shanelle."

I turned around and cut him a look like a woman possessed. "He's on top of his game tonight," I thought, as I stared down at a full tube of Crest. I just had ice cream so there was no need to force feed myself as I slowly brushed my teeth. Alex came into the bathroom, pretending to look for something. He brushed against me just to make his presence known.

"Looking for something?" I asked.

He stood behind me and placed his hands on my hips. After he kissed my neck he said, "My dental floss."

I picked it up and handed it to him. I took his other hand off my hip and walked out.

The heavy comforter was a quiet surrender for the night. I didn't want him to touch me anymore, even though I didn't want the feeling to last for long. Parts of me felt hurt on the inside. The other parts looked for repressed places to hide. Alex climbed into bed and snuggled next to me. He tugged and pulled on me until we fit like a perfect puzzle piece. I was still angry at him, but his touched softened the places that hurt as I closed my eyes. His antidote for the evening was not to be mad at me as he palmed my swollen stomach with his right hand. "I love you Shanelle," Alex said.

"I love you too Alex." I replied.

Back to Reality

It felt good to finally reach home. It was late when we arrived and Alex had to leave the following morning. He went through the mail and sorted mine into a small pile. I shuffled through the letters looking for my fall class schedule from St. James University. "Hey Alex, I got all of my classes."

"That's good," he replied. A phone call interrupted my moment. Alex answered in a deep tone as if he did not want to be bothered. "Hello." His voice changed at the sound of the caller's voice.

"What's up mom? Yeah, we just got in." His tone got softer. "I missed you too." He looked up at me and smiled. I loved his genuine affection for his mother. Although his next response was my demise from the both of them.

"A crib? It's a little early to be talking about that ma, besides we just got back from our honeymoon." I shifted through the letters again thinking, "That's right dammit, stop sweatin' a crib, ask me how I'm doing or something, shit, talk about the weather if you must." I laughed on the inside. I found it difficult to act like a new wife or a lady in waiting. Grandma was on the other line, setting up shop like I was starring in Rosemary's Baby.

"I'll look at it later." Alex replied. Alex hung up the phone and laughed. I knew he was going to say something.

"Can you believe my mother?" He asked. "She's already passing down antique baby furniture."

"I hate antique anything," I replied.

Alex cut me a look like I should have kept that comment to myself, but instead he took a deep breath. "Our baby is going to have brand new everything anyway." He stood behind me and wrapped his arms around my waist. "And you're going to need maternity clothes right?"

I pushed his hands away and snapped, "No!"

Alex looked at me like I was crazy and said, "Shanelle, you complained your clothes were too tight..."

I didn't let him finish. "Well, I'll just buy some bigger clothes." I pulled and tugged at my shirt in two different directions and then looked at the bathroom for sanctuary. "I need to pee." Alex rolled his eyes and said, "Thanks for sharing."

The full-length mirror behind the bathroom door was calling my name. I closed the door and immediately removed my clothes. After my eating fest in the Bahamas, I was curious to see the effect on my body. When I looked up, the image of myself fostered Alex's comment. To my horror, I looked like a swollen cow. There was no curvature to my waist. My breasts were swollen two times their original size and for the first time my thighs were stuck together. My shoulders sagged to enhance the disfigured image I saw in the mirror. In two short weeks, the tiny being inside of me and my uncontrollable eating habits now held my body hostage. Looking away for a minute offered no resolve as the voices began to giggle. I turned to the side and the laughter became louder. My ass ballooned out so big, I was sure Alex's nephews would ask for a ride sidesaddle. Better yet, an attraction at the local carnival.

"Step right up ladies and gentleman, get your three dollar ticket to see Shanelle's big ass."

I closed my eyes to think it away, but when I opened them, the ugly image was still there. "Damn," I thought, "How am I going to cover this shit up?" I got so angry, I contemplated breaking the mirror, but a small tap at the door quickly resolved that thought.

"Shanelle, are you okay in there?" In a defeated voice I replied, "I'm fine."

Alex's next question could have ignited world war three.

"That was a long trip, are you hungry?"

I mimicked his question with my lips, swaying my head to and fro, "Are you hungry are you hungry?" My hands rested on my hips in defense mode.

"Well?" He asked.

"No, I'm fat enough as it is."

Alex sucked his teeth and said, "Look, stop acting like a baby and come out of the bathroom."

"I'm not acting like a baby, I'm having one, remember?"

"Well, I'll tell you one thing, you're not going to get any smaller in there. Besides, I'm leaving in the morning and we need to go over some things."

I don't know why I did it, but I opened the door so Alex could see me in all of my fat naked glory. Alex started laughing and said, "You look good to me juicy girl, so don't think you're going to get any sympathy." He fell to his knees and kissed my stomach in ten places. "Hello Pumpy, it's me, Daddy."

I put my hand on his head and said, "Pumpy, where did that come from?" Alex looked up at me and said, "That's my son's nick name, I know he's going to be a big one." I looked up to the ceiling and said, "This is unreal." A smack on my butt followed as Alex replied, "Like I said, you'll be ok, mommy." He picked me up just to prove his manhood. "Damn girl, you're still a lightweight." We plopped on the couch. Alex took off his tee shirt and put it over my head. He knew I loved his scent, especially at the end of the day. Even after a smelly plane ride, I was still enticed by the touch smell of his clothes. More importantly, having him so close to me prompted the sadness I began to feel. The last thing I wanted him to do was leave. I cupped his face and kissed his lips as he spoke to me.

"Listen, don't forget to pay the cable and public service. Whatever expenses you need for school has to be paid by check. I left five hundred dollars for you in my dresser. Use the JC Penny credit card if you want to pick up bigger clothes." He winked at me as a comforting gesture.

"That's right," I replied, "Bigger clothes, not maternity clothes."

Alex cleared his throat and said, "Shanelle, I don't want you looking sloppy, like I don't take care of you. Make sure you buy some clothes. I'll call you in the morning on the road. Jack is going to drive so you can have the car while I'm gone." Alex paused for a minute and adjusted my ring back to center position. "I love you mommy and I want you to make a doctor's appointment tomorrow. If you have an emergency, call Captain Fisco, that's the only way you can reach me."

I tugged at his ear and said, "Promise me you'll be safe…, I've heard about friendly fire." Alex put his finger to my lips and said. "I'll be fine, don't worry, it's you I worry about. Will you go to my mother's if you get lonely; you can sleep in my old room. I've got tee shirts there too." I nestled my head in his neck and said, "I'll be fine." He knew I was lying. "Baby girl, a month will fly by so fast. Just keep yourself busy, you'll see."

I didn't say a word. I wanted him to stay, but I knew how much his job meant to him. His need to help others was part of his redemption.

We both took quick showers and climbed into bed in complete exhaustion. I remembered falling asleep worrying about him leaving me and the emptiness I would feel. Nestled in his embrace, I began to escape into a world of fretful dream sleep.

"One more game," Steven said, as he slammed down the game piece.

"No, I don't want to play Sorry anymore, I beat you fair and square."

His voice changed in tone, "Sit down, I said."

I looked at him and laughed, "Why don't you sit down you sore loser."

He jumped up and put me in a choke hold as I screamed for mercy. "Ok, ok, you won!" My plea of surrender didn't satisfy him as he gripped my neck.

"Who's the number one soul brother on the planet?" Steven yelled. His grip tightened around my neck as I gasped for small amounts of air. I replied, "You Steven, you're the number one soul brother." He mashed my head into the floor and kicked me in my butt. "You better not tell mommy either or I'll kick your ass real good the next time." My eyes rolled back into focus as Steven dragged me by my ankles into the living room and threw my feet to the floor. He slammed the door to the family room and said, "Don't come back either, Good Times is on and I want to see Jay Jay kick Thelma's ass too."

I rubbed my throat as I walked into the kitchen to make a pot of rice before Mrs. Viv got home. As soon as I stepped onto the black and white tile floor, I fell straight through into a dark and scary abyss. The sensation of falling began as I started to scream in mid air. I reached out my hands and called God for salvation.

"Help me God please." Suddenly, I stopped falling. I was in the embrace of Alex's strong arms.

"Shanelle, its ok, you were dreaming."

My heart was beating so fast that Alex placed his hand on my heart to reduce the tempo. "You're drenched too Shanelle." I took off my top as Alex got up and took a tee shirt out of the drawer. Even in my dazed state of confusion, Alex's presence calmed my fears. I put his tee shirt on and wrapped my arms around him. The clock suddenly became my enemy. Alex shifted his body weight and looked me in the eyes. "I've got to leave in two hours Shanelle and I didn't want to leave like this."

"It was just a bad dream," I replied.

"Steven?" Alex asked.

I scratched my head and told the truth. "Yeah, I always knew something was wrong with him because his temper just got worse over time." Alex sighed and slid his fingertips onto my scalp.

"Did he ever hit you?" The touch of his head massage induced a slow and steady answer. "No, I'm mean, yeah, but not punches, more like choking and pushing. I guess he knew that if he left a mark my parents would finally take my side."

Alex's fingers slowed down as he began to speak. He cleared his throat and said, "I made a few phone calls to a buddy of mine on the North Orange squad. I didn't get all of my info yet, but I want you to stay clear of your parents' house and the Garvey Projects. Especially Garvey, he made some serious enemies over there." Alex picked up my chin to hear my answer. "Ok?"

I grabbed his wrists to keep his hands in my hair and said, "Ok, I will."

Alex looked at the clock and said, "Damn." I squeezed him tight to confirm his sentiment.

"I wish you didn't have to go Alex. Who's going to hold me at night?" Alex tucked the sheet into me and held me tighter. "The maiden sighs today?" Alex asked.

"You did read it after all." I said.

"Yes, it was beautiful and I packed it in my bag with my favorite picture."

"The black and white bikini?"

"No, the one of you writing poetry, that's my favorite." Alex cleared his throat and said, "Not to change the subject Shanelle, but I feel terrible for leaving you. This is for us, so just hold on to me right now and remember this place. When I come home, we'll leave off where we started."

Early morning bad breath didn't stop our love. Alex put his hand under my back and enticed my hands onto his loins. A natural moan churned inside of me as my breasts began to ache. Alex put me on top of him as I took center stage. His face strained as he began to smile as my thighs worked a smooth and easy rhythm. This time he called my name as he grabbed my behind and sped up my pace. The swell of my stomach began to increase again as my forehead began to perspire. Alex teased me and said, "Look at my baby getting her skills up."

My thighs began to tremble into a full collapse as Alex took over. He rolled over on top of me and held my legs up. I bit into my lips as the strength of his body went through my back into ecstasy. Three more strokes and Alex was done. He looked at the clock and said, "Take a bath with me before I go."

The sunlight had yet to rise as we lit three candles and placed them inside the edges of the shower stall. We lit one for our love, one for our marriage. Alex lit the last one and said, "This one's for Pumpy." He kissed my forehead as we quietly slipped into the tub together. The hot water melted us into one soapy being. Alex slid his massive hands down my thighs and massaged them with long hard strokes. He claimed me by marking my back with a big ass hickey. Every now and then he held my hand up and stared at my wedding ring. I got out of the tub first and quietly donned some satin pajamas. I sat on the bed and watched him pack a few clothes. He put his favorite baseball cap on my head while he continued packing. He also wrapped his favorite pictures of me in tissue paper and put it in the side pocket of his travel bag. Watching him pack was unbearable as I crawled under our covers. I pulled his baseball cap down so he wouldn't see me crying. Before the sun rose, Alex slipped off to training with a kiss to my forehead as he carefully removed his hat from my head. He tucked the curly strands behind my ear and said, "I love you Shanelle, remember what I told you." He picked up my favorite teddy that he gave me on our first date and tucked it in my arms. "Hold him until I get back." Then he kissed my stomach and said, "Be good to mommy Pumpy."

I closed my eyes as fast tears continued to stream down my face. I didn't want to see him leave. He wasn't coming back at noon or tomorrow. Thirty days was too long for my heart or nerves to endure. It wasn't until I heard him close the door that the realization of my emptiness kicked in. I squeezed my teddy bear tight and quietly cried myself to sleep.

Busy Body

Surprisingly, after five hours of sleep, waking up at eleven a.m. felt pretty good. The phone rang and I knew it was Alex. "Hello."

"Hey baby," he said.

"Hey, where are you?"

"Just outside of Philly." Alex replied. "We just left a diner."

"Oh," I said. "Say hi to Jack for me."

"Ok," Alex said, "What are you doing today?"

"I don't know, but I'll stay busy like you said."

"Ok busy body, don't forget, Tammy's home for a few more days, maybe you can go to the beach with her." Alex said.

"Ok," I replied. The thought had not entered my mind and I really wasn't interested.

"I'll call you later," Alex said. "We're about to get back on the road. I love you, take some vitamins Shanelle and make a doctor's appointment."

"I love you too and I will," I replied.

We hung up and I looked around the room. The first thing I needed to do was find something to wear. I found a black sleeveless shirt and some black pedal pushers with an elastic waist for my expanding tummy. I packed a small bag with shorts, a tee shirt, Nike sneakers, a brush and some Nunile. I put some mascara on and pulled my hair back in a tight ponytail. The mirror smiled back at me today. Amazingly my skin was clear as a shiny button with no acne. A plot began to form in my brain. "Let me see what's up on my side of town." I grabbed three hundred dollars, the check book and my class schedule. The slam of the front door should have been a warning as I headed for the car. Alex left me with a full tank of gas and a roll of Parkway tokens. I put on my sunglasses and turned on Kiss FM. I bopped my head to the beat and kicked back in a female gangster lean as I sang, *"Hey dj just play that song, keep me dancing..."*

Eric B. and Rakim came on next as I put the car in first gear and headed out of Lakewood for some action.

First stop, St James University. I paid the 145 exit toll and decided to cruise through North Orange before I headed to the campus. I donned my sunglasses and headed down Oakwood Avenue. Kids with white tanks and shorts were running with basketballs to Garvey. I looked past the swell of the crowd headed toward Garvey Street. It was a cue that the summer league pick up games were in full swing. Without hesitation, I hung a right and headed for the Garvey projects. The same ole crew was out and about. I saw Big Booty Brenda, the local skank who knew everybody's business.

I called from the window and said, "Brenda, who's playing?" She walked up to the car to get a better look and said, "Hey Shanelle." Before Brenda answered, she did a full inventory search of the car as her fingers played a melody on the door. "Mookie's over there entertaining with his ugly ass." She pointed at me and said, "When you see Steven, tell him he better pay me my fuckin' money." I started shaking my head and said, "We don't conversate anymore." Brenda replied, "Conversate my ass, family is family, you'll see his tired ass at a fuckin' barbecue or something. Just tell him what I said please." Brenda rolled her eyes and turned her lip up as she pulled back. My face turned up as her funky smell lit up the entire car. It almost made me pass out as I looked for a parking space. She walked along the side of my car as sparks flew out the back of her shoes. Brenda stayed in worn out shoes with nails and curled up plastic rising up from the heel. "Damn," I thought, "You can light a cigarette from the back of those shoes." Brenda kept it movin' but rolled her eyes at me. She was probably pissed off with some Steven bullshit but I didn't care, because he wasn't my problem anymore. I got out the car and put my shades on the top of my head. I brought an Italian ice from Rockies and headed up the block for the game. The quad was packed to watch Mookie play in the hot asphalt sun. On the mini courts, little kids were practicing their skills in between the oohs and aahs of Mookie's game. Mookie had good game too. In the heart of the projects, the swell of the crowd was black, Puerto Rican and some wannabees. The weird thing was watching old men in khaki pants with press pads in their hands hungrily waiting to recruit Mookie. They took notes and stood in separate huddles calculating the lure it would take to get him to Villanova, Duke, Marquette, you name it, they were there. They were going to have to work hard too. His mother, "Mama Barb," as we called her, made sure her baby stayed out of trouble and ate a good meal. She fed the whole damn neighborhood too. The good heart she had did little for Mookie's education, but she made sure that nobody went hungry. She sold five dollar chicken dinners from her apartment five days a week and gave the Peppermint a run for their money. Mama Barb always said that chicken and rice came cheap. People trusted her food too because she kept a clean apartment and a white dishrag continuously soaking in bleach. Amazingly, she managed to keep every roach in the project out of her place with monthly boric acid treatments. My stomach started growling just thinking about her perfect white rice and brown gravy. On a hot ass day like today, you would think that all I wanted was coconut Italian ice, but I moved through the crowd and rolled right up on Mama Barb to buy an early dinner. "Hey Shanelle, go help yourself," she said, as I handed her some money. The rest of the cash I flashed was a mistake, because sticky finger Tamika walked up to me to get a piece. She grabbed my ring finger as I shoved my wad into my pocket.

"Damn, you doing aight' girl with that ring on your finger." A good compliment came first, then a pitiful story to get some money. "Look here," she said, as she wiped her nose, "I need to get some bread and milk for my kids, can you loan me twenty?"

Never look a feign in the eye, my brother used to say. If you do, they'll spot your weakness and be your friend for life. I looked straight ahead and picked up my plate. One scoop of rice and gravy went in mouth as I said, "I calculate two dollars and forty-five cents, what are you gonna do with the change?" Tamika quickly sucked her teeth. My question, the food in my mouth and the hot swell of the sun pissed her off as she walked away. "Oh, forget you Shanelle, your brother owes me some money, you better tell him to come see my ass."

"Yeah whatever," was my response. I scooped up some more rice and looked around. The true basketball heads were fixated on Mookie and his legendary slam-dunks. There were others with different intentions. Among the crowd were bookies, gun-runners, pimps in training and hookers in heels. Little did I know federal agents were staked out in apartment 7H shooting rapid fire photographs of the entire spectacle. Vehicles parked along the side were also subject to evidence and inventory. Lucky me, they even took a photograph of me biting into a chicken leg as one of the most ruthless crime suspects walked up to me in the crowd.

"Yo, Shanelle, what's up?"

"Hey Rico, nothing much."

"You kinda far from Seven Oaks."

"I don't live there anymore and it's not Seven Oaks," I replied. The chicken melted down my throat as my heart began to thump in my shirt. I knew what was coming next.

"Look, you know I always had a crush on you girl and I'm always gonna look out for you. You need to step because Steven made some crazy enemies up in here and everybody's lookin' for him."

The last swallow was a hard gulp as I tried to avoid the subject. "How's Nikki doing?"

"Good," Rico replied. "At least she made it out, she's a varsity point guard at Pitt."

Nikki and Rico's parents had enough sense to keep their daughter in St. Amelia's for as long as their five jobs could carry them. We weren't that cool in high school, but I was happy for her because she was a good ball player. I threw my plate in the garbage as I licked my lips. "Let me get up outta here."

Rico replied, "Yeah, you do that and tell mama boy Steven to come see me."

I walked to the car with keys in hand and never looked back. "Damn," I thought, "Steven really fucked up." I rolled up the windows and headed towards Scotland Road. I needed to make a quick stop at Shoprite before I went back home. I nixed the thought of going to the university because of the intense heat outside.

As soon as I walked in Shoprite, I knew I was missed. Gina the sales clerk spotted me the minute I walked in the store.

"Shanelle, long time no see! I hear you're married now!"

The other cashier Maria chimed in too. "Yeah, she even put on honeymoon weight, look how happy she looks."

"Hi, Gina," I replied. "Yes, I'm a fat old married

woman."

Maria added her two cents as she continued to tally her order. "Your mother is here somewhere, I think down aisle two."

I was in no condition to run away as I turned my head in her direction. Curiosity pulled me right in as I began to slowly walk towards the aisle. A quick glance was all I needed to spot Mrs. Viv. She was looking at a can of Alpo holding a small basket in her hand. My body hardened for a moment as I gathered up the courage to face her. She was humming her all time favorite.

"I'm coming up, on the rough side…" I finished the verse as I walked up behind her and sang, "Of the mountain. I'm doing my best to make it in." I also chimed in as she turned around, "Hi mama."

"Shanelle," she said with sheer surprise, "My baby, how are you?" Before I could answer, she engulfed me in a back breaking squeeze. I embraced her as far as my arms could reach as my body melted in the her arms.

"I'm fine mama, I'm fine." She continued to hug me as she smoothed out my back in a nurturing exchange. After that, suspicion set in as she softly pushed me back.

"Look at you, all grown up and married now."

I showed her my ring as she held my hand and surveyed my mid section.

"Hmm," she said, "I see, I see. "How are you feeling?" Mrs. Viv asked.

"Fine mama," I replied, as I grabbed her basket and put it on the floor. The contents inside surprised me. Ramen noodles, one onion, two bananas and a loaf of bread. The selection was highly unusual because Mrs. Viv always had a cartful of groceries. I pointed at the basket and said, "You don't usually buy this stuff."

Mrs. Viv's face turned into a frown.

"Shanelle, I lost my job eight months ago and things

have been rough. I'm still looking though... even sending out resumes, but it's been hard. Your father got laid off too and he's doing free lance work right now."

I didn't dare ask about Steven and I really didn't care. It was all Mrs.Viv needed to say as I reached in my pocket for money.

I pulled out a one hundred dollar bill and handed it to her. "Here mama." She took the bill and folded it in half. After that she looked around and slipped it in her bra the old school way.

"Thank you baby..." Her pause was the first step in our healing. "I'm sorry Shanelle..."

I stroked her cheek with my hand to suspend her apology. It was all I could do to fight back tears. "I know mama, you did the best you could do, don't worry about it I'll be fine."

Tears welled up in her eyes as she desperately asked, "Can I call you Shanelle?" Mrs. Viv's face was full of expression. "You know, at your home. I don't know if you're getting my messages at Candy's house and I found out from a complete stranger that you got married."

I'm sorry mama, we came by to tell you the good news, but you weren't home." As I pulled out a pen, Mrs. Viv reached into her bosom for the money.

"Write it on here, I want to show your father when I get home." She paused for a second and then said, "He'll be so happy when I tell him I saw you." She snapped her fingers and asked, "Can you stop at the house, your father would love to see you."

A sharp sensation washed over me as I suddenly remembered the promise I made to Alex. "I'm sorry mama, I gotta get back to Lakewood."

Mrs. Viv's face washed over with sadness as I scribbled my name and number on the bill and handed it back to her. She reached into her shirt and buried the money back into her breast as she exhaled out loud. My rejection put her on the defensive as she stared me up and down, paying astute attention to my stomach. She tugged on my shirt and said, "You're pregnant Shanelle."

My mouth dropped to the ground as I stood back and stuttered, "How, how did you…"

She stepped towards me and touched my cheek and said something I would quickly regret.

"Looking at you is like looking at me when I was pregnant with Steven, you must be having a boy." She continued to speak, but everything she said began to take on a hollow tone as I drifted away…

"Steven made me swell up the minute I got pregnant with him. I think I was in maternity clothes at four weeks. My stomach swelled up so bad, your grandmother had to add elastic in the waist of my pants just so I could go out. Oooh girl, I ate like a pig too, anything I could get my hands on…." She turned my chin towards her and said, "Shanelle, are you all right?"

My voice became deep and demonic as I finally took ownership of the life growing inside of me. "Does everything have to be about Steven? This baby isn't going to be anything like him mama, I mean it, so don't go putting Steven into my pregnancy." When I finished, I embraced my small pouch with a gentle and caring embrace. Before this day came, I was wishing the entire reality away. Mentioning Steven was like drawing a battle line. I was more than determined to win this war no matter what. A drum majorette played a tune in my head as I stood up straight and fixed my clothes. Loose strands of hair were quickly swept to the side of my hair line as I looked at her in complete defiance.

Mrs. Viv didn't raise a white flag, but she did offer one suggestion of peace.

"I'm sorry baby, I wasn't trying to do that. Did you

see a doctor yet, I can make an appointment for you…"

I hugged her quickly and began to walk away. Avoidance was the only way I could deal with my past ordeal. "I have to go mama, the parkway traffic gets busy at this time. I'll call you later." With that, I scurried out the door and jumped in the car. As soon as I sat down in Alex's bucket seats, the sensation to go to the bathroom overwhelmed me. I immediately looked around and and decided to go to the Exxon station. Once inside, I released what felt like a gallon of fluid. The relief was so overwhelming after I washed my hands that I had to stand outside to catch my breath. I put my hands on my hips and looked at the blinking light on top of the VA Hospital. I also stared at the phone booth that used to be my haven when I ran away. Memories came back to me as I reflected.

"Steven, whose wallets are these and where did you get these watches from?"

"Stay outta my shit fat ass".

"Well, you left them on the table, I didn't know."

"You don't know shit, that's your problem. You need to grow up, shit, smoke a joint or somethin'."

"Steven, the doctor said you shouldn't smoke that stuff…"

I shut my eyes as I visualized his physical response. One hard push sent me flying into the mirrored wall as my head broke a precut glass diamond that lodged into my head.

"Oww, look what you did Steven, I'm bleeding!"

"So what! At least your head is not all fucked up inside, so quit your fucking whining Shanelle before I show ma those love letters under your bed for Derrick you horny bitch!"

The squawk of a black crow snapped me out of my trance as I looked up in the sky. The need to eat again started to overwhelm my taste buds and stomach as I pulled out of the gas station, anxious to finally reach home.

It took me two hours to get back to Lakewood. Once inside, I immediately noticed two phone messages. One from Mrs. Foster and one from Alex's sister Tammy. "Let the games begin," I thought, while I listened to Mrs. Foster carry on about her new grandbaby.

"And I saw the cutest little outfit today Shanelle, I was tempted to buy it…Anyway, I thought you would be home resting, but it is a nice day. I brought you some vitamins from the store and some orange juice, folic acid is good for the baby you know. Well anyway, call me, I want you to look at this darling crib."

The next message was Tammy. She wanted me to join the chubby club.

"Hey girl, I was going to pick you up for lunch and then I thought we could swing to Belmar. I'm going to Lane Bryant's tomorrow if you want to go, so let me know, bye."

The delete key was the only way out. Sure I got the message, but I wasn't thrilled about either one of them. Thoughts of my mother quickly rested in my mind as I looked down at my belly. "This baby won't be anything like Steven," I thought, as I grabbed the phone book. The first thing I needed to do was make sure my baby was okay. I sat on the couch and scrawled my finger down the list. "Hmm, Dr. Cathy Johnson, she sounds nice," I thought.

"Dr. Johnson's office, may I help you?"

"Yes, uh, hi, this is…"

"Can you hold on please, thanks."

Waiting, waiting, waiting, elevator music, waiting…

"Hi, can I help you?"

"This is Shanelle Brown, uh, I mean, Mrs. Shanelle Foster, I need to make an appointment.

"What insurance do you have?"

"Oh, I just got married and I don't think my husband added me on…"

"Well the office visit is two hundred and fifteen dollars without it and that doesn't include blood work."

I didn't know what to say or do, Alex didn't say to spend the money at the doctor's office.

"Hello, are you there Miss?"

"Yes, I'm here, I'll call back, thank you." "Well," I thought to myself, "I tried."

I quickly jumped off the couch and took a shower. As I stepped out, the scale was the first thing that came into eyesight. I avoided it in the worst way, but the swell of my stomach and baby talk by the world around me forced me to check my weight. I placed my right foot slowly on the scale, being ever so careful to place it in the center. As my left foot released the floor, the numbers quickly shot past one hundred and sixty pounds. I quickly stepped down as my heart began to beat in rapid successions. "That can't be," I thought. This time I put my left foot on the scale and added my right foot. When I looked down, to my horror, the scale read one hundred and sixty-seven pounds.

"How could that be?" I thought, as I took my towel off. I stepped on the scale again and the numbers appeared in the glass display again.

"Step right up ladies and gentleman and look at the fat freak show." I don't know which one of the voices said it, but I quickly left the bathroom and ran into the bedroom. I grabbed one of Alex's tee shirts and laid across the bed as I cried. My fingers felt like fat swollen sausages as I wiped my tears away. Nothing soothed my thoughts as I contemplated eating peanut butter. I cried so hard that I eventually fell asleep. Even if I wanted to get up and eat something, all the excitement from the afternoon forced me to sleep. By nightfall, emotional wreckage followed.

Ring, ring, ring, ring, ring, ring, ring…

"Hello," I said.

"Shanelle, it's me."

"Alex?"

"Yes, it's Alex, are you sleeping?"

A smile overwhelmed my face as I grabbed the phone cord.

"I was, but I'm up now."

In a hostile and angry tone, he cleared his throat and said, "Where did you go today?"

I cleared my throat, clueless to his line of questioning. "Oh, uh… I went to North Orange, I was going to check on my courses but…oh, I got something to eat, oh yeah, I saw…"

"I didn't ask you who you saw Shanelle, I asked where did you go?" An official police interrogation set in as my eyes shifted back and forth in our dark bedroom. Quickly trying to recall, my eyebrows began to burrow into a serious expression. "Let me think, I went to Sandwiches Unlimited, no, not there, I mean Shoprite. Uh, I watched some basketball…"

"Yeah, that's it," Alex said, "Tell me about basketball."

My heart began to sink to the ground as I contemplated my error. "Mookie was playing…"

"Mookie?" Alex asked with a sarcastic tone in his voice. "What the fuck is a Mookie?" No, better yet Shanelle, tell me where he was playing basketball."

I stuttered briefly as I replied, "Garvey."

Alex yelled like a drill sergeant. "Garvey what?"

"Uh, Garvey Street Projects," I replied, as I tucked my pillow under my arms.

Alex began to scream at me in a wild tirade, "Yeah, that's the answer I was looking for Shanelle, Garvey Street Projects, the very place I told you not to go!"

As Alex's wrath fell upon me in decorated black silk, all I could here was the sound of tapping. I didn't know if he was in a phone booth or in a hotel room, but déjà vu came into being. Alex's response swept me in a dark wind tunnel as he yelled at me.

"Before I left, I specifically said not to go to your parents' house or the Garvey Street Projects! Why did my captain call me in the middle of training and say that my license plate showed up on a federal evidence stake out list? For your information Shanelle, the feds are over there taking pictures of every car, bookie, gun runner, drug dealer and wanna be gangsters. Never in a million years would I expect my wife to show up in those pictures eating a fucking two piece chicken dinner and talking to the number one suspect in their investigation!"

The wind tunnel swept me up as chicken bones, marrow and unearthly debris rested on my lifeless body. "Garvey, chicken, Mookie, Rico, who knew?" Alex's rage continued as I listened to Alex's alter ego blare into the phone.

"Did you forget I'm a cop? Did you forget you're my wife, more importantly, did you forget you're pregnant and you had the damn audacity to show up at that crime infested neighborhood!" Alex began to laugh as Jack stood in the back ground trying to calm him down.

"No man, get off of me, she needs to hear this. Shanelle, do you know that I am a laughing stock around here because my wife thinks she's a home girl! Do you know you damn near made me lose my job?"

I was frozen on the bed as I listened to him.

"Shanelle, this is our entire life. If I lose this job, we all lose. What the hell were you thinking?"

I couldn't speak nor was it time to respond.

"You better be glad Captain Fisco likes me and called in a favor, but now I'm fucked trying to figure out how I'm going to pay it back. But for now, I want you to do me a favor Mrs. Foster." His demand bellowed through my hollow body.

"Get up off the bed and look out the window."

I couldn't move.

"Did you hear what I said?" He asked.

"Yes Alex."

"Get up and go to the living room window now!"

I jumped up and quickly walked to the window in my bare feet.

"I'm here," I said, in a timid voice.

"Good, now lift up the blind, Shanelle."

Darkness settled outside as I stared at the parking lot.

"Are you looking?" he asked.

"Yes," I responded.

"See anything missing?" Alex asked.

I was clueless. His anger forced a response.

"Look at our parking space, number thirty-five!"

My eyes quickly shifted to our space as my heart sunk to the ground. "Uh, the car, it's…"

"Gone!" Alex yelled, "Gone!" That's the deal I made with Captain Fisco and the Feds to keep you out of North Orange until this part of the investigation is over! Now you can stay at home and act like my wife instead of trying to front like some project girl!" His tirade wasn't over as he shifted to his prodigy. "Did you make an appointment today?"

"I tried but I didn't have…"

"Not good enough Shanelle, you've got time to watch somebody name Mookie, but no time for our baby. Be ready by nine o'clock tomorrow, my mother is picking you up for an appointment with Dr. Robinson."

Thoughts of his unborn child seemed to calm his voice. He cleared his throat and said, "How are you feeling?"

My response was weak and filled with hurt. "Fine," I replied.

His next question was a test of my will on any given day. "Are you eating?" Alex asked.

Tucked away in the deepest shame, my tearful voice said, "Yes, I'm eating."

Alex cleared his throat in sheer sarcasm and said, "Oh I forgot, you had fried chicken today. Anyway, be ready in the morning." What followed was the blaring sound of the dial tone as I held the phone in sheer shock and embarrassment. I quietly looked around the room as the voices gathered around me with sticks and torches, ready to burn Frankenstein at the stake.

"No he didn't," The Big One said.

"Yes he did," The Meek One retorted.

"He got some nerve talkin' to you like that."

"Who does he think he is, Steven or something?"

My body rocked back and forth as I held my ears tight. The sheets on the bed became a handkerchief as I buried my head deep inside the soft cloth and bellowed out in shame and humiliation. Suddenly, the phone rang again. Eternal hope rested for a quick minute as I heard the third ring. "Please tell me you forgive me Alex," I wiped away my wet hands on my thighs and slowly picked up the phone. The sound coming from the receiver offered little hope as the voice of Steven came on loud and clear singing an awful rendition of Maurice White from Earth, Wind and Fire.

Ohhh, ohh, oh, after the love is gone, what use to be right is wrong.... Ha haaaa, what's up little sis, and better yet how's my little nigga nephew in that big ass belly of yours?"

My body tensed up in pure fear and anxiety as I tried to control the pitch in my voice. "How did you get my number Steven?"

His voice had complete control as he replied, "The hooker that you are wrote it on that hundred spot you gave ma. Thanks for the get high money dummy." Laughter rang out through the ear piece as I quickly hung up the phone. Steven wasn't finished, he was on a roll. In five minutes, the phone rang again. I knew it was Steven, but I couldn't take the chance if it was Alex. I needed to tell Alex that I was sorry.

"Hello."

"Hey Nell," Steven said, "Can you imagine my big head nephew runnin' around the house, I'm so excited, you know I can't wait to pop that little nigga in the back of his big ass head."

I rubbed my stomach like a she wolf protecting her young. Mrs. Viv did even more damage to my psyche by telling him that I was pregnant. I hung up the phone and quickly called back. Mrs. Viv and Steven picked up the phone as I began to yell. "Stop calling here Steven and leave me alone!" The buffer between us was one hundred and thirty miles. It was the first time in a long time that Mrs. Viv took my side.

"Steven, leave your sister alone!" There was desperation in her voice as she called my name.

"Shanelle, Shanelle, are you there?" I immediately hung up and quickly ran to the bathroom for sanctuary. The voices were right behind me in thought as I began to press against my stomach with the palm of my hands. "No, no, no, I don't want you to be like him, please God, don't do this to me." Tears began to fall uncontrollably. I forced myself off the floor and went into the kitchen. Among the cabinets and the refrigerator were the things I craved in times of stress. Work had to be done because Alex made sure that healthy food remained in the house. My mind shifted into hyper overdrive as I grabbed the peanut butter and three bananas. I held them tightly under my right arm as I opened the door to the refrigerator. Cream cheese, goat cheese and left over fat free pudding were snatched from the first shelf. I topped it off with a half-gallon container of milk. With all of the contents tightly wrapped in my arms, I headed for the bathroom and closed the door. Under the evening twilight, on the cold ceramic floor, my sneaky eating device gripped my soul. Peanut butter and cream cheese went down first as I forced hard swallows to calm my stress. The bananas followed in perfect unison as I took one bite and swallowed it whole. Sweat tremors kicked in and a small dizzy spell followed as my existence filled the entire bathroom with voices of shame.

"You're stupid, fat and worthless. How could you be so stupid? Will you ever listen? Hide in the closet where you can't be seen or heard. He's going to kill you anyway. Who? Alex? No, Steven. Well, maybe Alex, he's killed before. Steven would if you gave him a chance. Maybe Alex could kill Steven and then you can be rid of Steven. But then Alex may kill you just so he can have the baby all to himself, that's all he wants. This baby won't be sick like Steven. Yes he will as soon as he pops the little one in the back of his head, he'll be crazy too."

I swallowed hard as I cursed them. Food began to fly out of my mouth in a pasty substance as I cursed myself. The pudding went down swift and steady as I spread my legs and licked the creamy residue dripping between each finger. There was no need to use utensils. My hands were the quickest release. Goat cheese and milk followed last. The milk dripped from my mouth and down my neck like a slow moving volcanic eruption as my heartbeat began to slow down. As the frenzy began to settle, my right hand slumped to the floor. My left hand soon followed and fell on the slump of my swollen stomach. My head rolled down in exhaustion. The only support was the toilet bowl beside me as my shoulder rested against the cold tile. The perspiration of the toilet bowl induced me into a cool calm. Finally the voices settled into a whisper as I took slow deep breaths.

"There there Shanelle, you're going to be fine. Alex

*won't kill you, he loves you, maybe too much, but he loves
you. Listen to him, he knows what's best for you. You're still
a little girl, lost in Alex's world."*

My body heaved up and down with two breaths of
air as my eyes began to close. I was hung over like a scene
from Lady Sings the Blues. Tears rolled down my cheek as
the still of the night silenced my vice and accompanied me
to sleep. Before I knew it, I surrendered to a dream.

"Shanelle, open the door, it's me!"

"Steven, what is it now?"

"Open the door, they're after me!"

"Quick, hide with me Shanelle!"

"Not in the closet again Steven!"

"Shh!"

"Steven, let go of me, there's nobody out there."

"They're trying to kill me sis!"

"Steven, don't cry, nobody is going to kill you."

"They chase me all the time Shanelle."

"Who?"

"The voices in my head."

"Why don't you tell ma..."

"No, they'll put me away, I'm not crazy!"

*"That's why you need to take your medicine. They'll
go away if you do. I know, you're not crazy... shh, shh,
there, there, Steven, you're going to be alright."*

"Don't leave me sis, don't let them get me."

"I won't, they won't get you, I promise."

A soft shoulder rub awakened me as I opened my
eyes. I blinked in wonderment as shoes in various forms
stood on the bathroom floor. My clothes were stuck to my
body like hard sticky paste as I looked at the remnants of
yogurt and milk stuck to my full framed body. As I blinked
my eyes into clearer focus, Mrs. Foster immediately took
control.

"Tammy, wait outside. Mary, you clean this mess up

and Debbie, help me get this child off the floor. Shanelle, can you hear me?"

I sat up and looked around at the Foster women.

"What time is it?"

"Girl, it's nine fifteen, you didn't answer the doorbell so we got worried and let ourselves in. Alex gave me a key before he left."

Mary picked up the cream cheese wrapper with a warm and loving smile. Forgiveness seemed to be her personality.

"Wow, Shanelle, you're really eating for two. My niece or nephew will be as strong as a bull, bananas are high in potassium."

Mrs. Foster held me by the shoulders and said, "Did you forget your appointment?"

"No," I replied.

Mary chimed in and said, "Ma you know that's the best sleep ever, especially the first trimester. Shanelle, do you want me to iron something for you?"

"Sure, uh, no problem, my jeans are in the dresser." I ran my fingers through my hair and looked at the Foster women clean up my demise. I was too tired to care, but I knew that Mrs. Foster was going to tell Alex about what she saw. I walked outside and saw Tammy sitting on the couch. Her face was as shameful as mine. She quickly said hello and put her head down in silence. I was sure she understood what I was going through.

I took a quick shower and toweled off. The phone rang and I quickly ran out of the bathroom to answer it but Mrs. Foster was on the phone. "Sure baby, I'll take care of it. Yes, we're leaving for the doctor's office the minute she gets dressed."

I reached out my hand for the phone, but Mrs. Foster hung it up. She looked at me with compassion in her eyes and said, "That was Alex, he was worried and took a break from training, he said he'll call you tonight at ten."

My hand fell to my side like a weighted stone. Mary handed me my jeans and a white tee shirt.

"Here you go Shanelle, this looks cute together." I grabbed the clothes and headed to the bathroom. The door closed behind me as they sat quietly in the living room. I didn't know what to think or to say, but I knew I needed to get to Dr. Robinson's office. I didn't want to disappoint Alex and I was determined to get this baby off to a good start. Steven's psychotic intentions forced me to worry about the innocent life inside of me as I brushed my teeth. I tapped my toothbrush and immediately thought of Alex. He was tapping something last night and it bothered me just like Steven's deadly blades. I slipped into my clothes and brushed my hair back into a ponytail. As I stepped out of the bathroom, the Foster women stood up to receive me with glowing compliments. It all sounded staged and rehearsed.

"You look great Shanelle," Tammy said, "You don't look fat at all." Mrs. Foster nudged Tammy with her elbow.

"Not fat at all," Mrs. Foster said, "My grandbaby is going to take of all of your weight anyway." Mrs. Foster grabbed my hand and squeezed it tight. "I made you some toast and wrapped it in some foil so you can have something on your stomach ok?"

The kindness she bestowed upon me made the embarrassment of my eating frenzy wash away.

"Ok." I replied.

"Good," Mrs. Foster said, "Let's get you to Dr. Robinson."

Dr. Robinson was a kind and caring woman. She made them wait in the reception area and spoke to me regarding my results. "Shanelle, you're in good health and from the looks of things you are definitely pregnant, five weeks to be exact. Your due date is April twenty-seventh. In the meantime, I would like to see you in two weeks so we can listen to the heartbeat." She handed me a prescription and said, "This is a prescription for prenatal vitamins. You should take them everyday with food. Do you have any questions?"

I had lots of questions, but none of them had to do with prenatal care. I looked down at my stomach and wished Steven away.

"No, I don't have any questions. Thank you Doctor Robinson."

"Help yourself to the magazines in the reception area. Prenatal care is very important Shanelle and those magazines offer helpful information. Please call me if you experience any bleeding or cramping."

I stood up, shook her hand and replied, "I'll see you in two weeks." I walked back to the reception area to get some magazines. Mary, Mrs. Foster and Tammy stood up to get all the details as I scoured the magazine rack.

"Is everything ok?" Tammy asked.

"How many weeks are you?" Mary inquired. As Debbie leaned in for a response, Mrs. Foster quickly got them off my back and grabbed two magazines. She kept one for herself and handed one to me.

"It's been a while since I had a grandbaby around so I'd better read myself, right Shanelle?"

I took the magazine from her and smiled. "Yeah, you're right Mrs. Foster."

She put her hand on my shoulder and said, "If you don't mind, call me mom, I would enjoy that."

I looked at Tammy and Mary and their eyes looked like it was a great sisterly suggestion. There was no way I could replace them as daughters, but as long as they didn't mind, I was willing to try. "Sure, I would love to call you mom."

Mrs. Foster drove back to her house. I could not refuse a dinner invitation and I wanted to keep busy until

Alex called. Tammy kept me company the whole time as we relaxed on her bed. She showed me all the new clothes she brought for school and we went over her class schedule. When she sat next to me on the bed, the mattress gave way and our shoulders touched in a sisterly bond.

"At least you can blame your pregnancy Shanelle."

"Blame my pregnancy? On what?"

Tammy looked at me and said, "You know, the eating thing."

I turned away and looked at the posters of New Edition on her wall. "I don't do it too much, but when I get…"

Tammy finished my sentence, "Upset, me too and I don't know how to stop.

I looked her in the eyes and said, "That was so embarrassing this morning."

There were tears in Tammy's eyes when she spoke. "It doesn't matter in this house, they've been through it with me too Shanelle, you just have to learn how to control it when things get out of wack you know?"

"Well," I asked. "What do you do to stop?"

Tammy replied, "The best thing is to stop and focus on a different task that keeps me busy like playing basketball or taking a walk. I mean, you can look at me and tell it doesn't work that much, but I've been heavier than this. If it weren't for Alex's motivation, I would be worse."

In complete curiosity I asked, "How did Alex help you?"

Tammy cleared her throat and sat with her legs crossed on her bed. "Alex is driven in everything he does. He's an over achiever if you didn't already know. I'm the same way except for one big problem."

"What's that?" I asked.

"I let other people influence me."

"Oh." I replied.

"I'm getting ready to go to Pitt and I know I'm weak. The minute somebody acts like they are my friend, I'm bending over backwards getting my feelings hurt. After that, I start binging the minute I feel anxious or stressed."

I didn't want to chime in and say, "me too," but I knew exactly how she was feeling.

"Alex talks to me all the time Shanelle, just to keep me moving. Before he met you, we used to run a mile on the beach or he would take me with him to the gym, just to keep busy. I only have one good friend and she moved to California last year. Hopefully I'll meet some cool people at Pitt."

I smiled at her and said, "I'm sure you will, hey, there's a girl I went to school with name Nikki who plays on the basketball team, you should hook up." I patted her leg and said, "I'm sure you'll find a nice guy too, you're cute as a button Tammy."

Tammy smiled and hugged me. "I was so jealous of you at first Shanelle, but I'm glad you're my sister now."

I hugged her back in relief and said, "Me too." It was a nice moment to share before dinner. We walked downstairs side by side as Tammy pushed me with her big hips at the last step. Mrs. Foster smiled at the two of us as she carried a steaming bowl of string beans to the table.

"Shanelle and Tammy, set the table for me please while I get this salad together."

In unison we chimed, "Ok mom." There was loud laughter between the two of us as we claimed her together. I felt so good being there I forgot all the problems that followed me the day before.

We all gathered around the table for prayer and thanked God for keeping Alex safe during his training. Tammy and I kept watch over our servings and winked at each other for making healthy choices like a big salad and no biscuits. We cleaned up after dinner and took a walk with

Mary and Alex's nephew. Once the night began to fall, I asked the same question over and over again.

"What time is it?"

Mrs. Foster said, "Lord somebody get this child home so she doesn't miss Alex's call." I chuckled at her response, but I was nervous just the same. Not talking to him was driving me crazy and I could not imagine what he was going to say to me.

Mary dropped me off and I quickly rushed to the door after saying goodnight. To my surprise, I quickly noticed a soft illuminating light from the bedroom. I looked up and immediately saw Alex sitting on the couch with a small duffel bag next to the couch. He looked up at me with no emotion on his face as I slowly walked towards him. He lifted his hand up so I could grab it as he pulled me between his legs and rested his head on my stomach. I immediately caressed his head as he exhaled.

"I'm sorry Shanelle," Alex said.

His words melted me into complete agreement. "I'm sorry Alex for not listening to you, what happened, I thought you were going to call me?"

"They suspended my training and want us to come in for questioning."

I pulled his head up and said in a quick and anxious voice, "Why?"

Alex exhaled out of disgust and said, "They want to know what you know about the people you were talking to in the photographs. Once their satisfied, I can go back to the training. They think you might be very helpful in their investigation." Alex sucked his teeth and said, "I wish you didn't have to Shanelle, but my job is on the line now."

I came up with every excuse I could think of and said, "I only know them from the neighborhood and school, I don't associate with them."

Alex quieted me with his fingertips and said, "I

know baby, I told them that, but this is a big case and they don't want to make the wrong move. I just need you to be honest with them and we'll be fine, it's just a formality." Alex cleared his throat and grabbed my hips to straddle his lap. I wrapped my legs around him as he looked me in the eyes and said, "How's Pumpy?"

I looked down at my stomach and said, "He or she is fine. I'm five weeks pregnant."

The smile on his handsome face stretched from ear to ear as all of his worries left his body. "You look cute mommy."

"Thank you," I replied.

"What did Dr. Robinson say?" He asked.

"She said everything was fine and she wanted to see me in two weeks to hear the heart beat."

Alex smiled again as he stroked my stomach with his thumbs. "Make sure you remind me about the date. I'm going to drive all the way back from Philly just to hear it."

"So you're not going to lose your job?" I asked.

Alex faced burrowed with worry as he squeezed my hand. "No Shanelle and I don't want to talk about it anymore, it's just a formality." He paused and said, "Look girl, I'll walk to the ends of the earth for you. I don't want you involved in this investigation and I don't need any attention on my life. You know why Shanelle. I told you my whole life story and I'm trying to make good on the things I did wrong in the past."

I couldn't do anything but apologize but he wouldn't let me. He laid me on down on the couch and stared at me. He grabbed my leg that was resting behind his back and placed them on his legs as he stroked my breasts and neck. His hands were so powerful, he could have easily popped my neck and ended my life right there. I squeezed my eyes tight as I tried to wrestle the thoughts away. Alex began to unbutton my shirt as I stared at him. His cinnamon skin looked so peaceful as he stroked the places I craved. Alex rubbed my stomach carefully sweeping his thumb under the seam of my panties as I began to arch my back. I asked him to take a shower with me but he refused.

"I told you before I left that we were going to finish where we left off. We can take a shower later." He pulled me up as I straddled his legs and began to unbutton his shirt. His skin was smooth to the touch as my nipples hardened again. He pulled me in closer to him and whispered in my ear. "I want you right now Shanelle."

I looked in his eyes and wondered if I should say something. I thought he wanted to go in the bedroom but perhaps he couldn't wait. I unbuckled his pants as he sat up for me to pull them down to his ankles. There was nothing left for me to do but to slide my tongue in his mouth as he sat me on top of his manhood. His face melted with pleasure as he sucked on my tongue in ecstasy. I pulled away from his mouth and stuck my tongue in his ear while calling his name. Alex grabbed my hips and worked my rhythm in a fast and furious pace as he called my name. His head rested back for a minute as he closed his eyes in complete pleasure. Alex wrapped four fingers around my thighs and worked Kitty with his thumb until my legs began to buckle beneath him. I started to cry as he forced me into creamy pleasure. He lifted me off of him and stepped out of his pants as he carried me to the bed and nestled his face between my legs. I screamed his name as more tremors released from within. Alex entered me again and cursed his own pleasure. "Damn girl, I love you so much." The side of his face was riddled with sweat as I cried for him. The feeling was so intense there was no way I could hold it in as he kissed away my tears. Alex got on his knees and rested my legs on his shoulders as he began to work his rhythm into another hurried frenzy. He finally surrendered in one big heap on top of me, carefully avoiding pressure on my

stomach. My legs fell on the bed in a rag doll slump as all
the energy left my body. A few shivers ran up my arm and
on to my shoulders as Alex rolled over. He pulled me into
him and threw the sheet over us as he kissed my neck.

"Just like I said, I was coming back just where we
left off."

My breathing calmed down as I turned into his chest
and wrapped my arms around him. "I'm so sorry for
everything."

Alex stroked my hair and said, "Go to sleep
Shanelle, we're going to be okay." I did go to sleep, but my
dreams forced me into thoughts of the next day.

*"Have a seat Mrs. Foster. I'm Special Agent
William, Truck Hijacking Squad, to your left Special Agent
Daniels, Fugitive Warrant Squad, next to Agent Daniels,
Special Agent Phillips, Narcotics Task Force. Seated on
your right, Special Agent Duncan, Evidence Agent and
photographer, who by the way took those lovely pictures of
you eating a five dollar two piece dinner at the Garvey
Projects. So, Mrs. Foster, tell me about Steven?"*

"I don't want to talk about him?"

*"Are you saying you are not going to cooperate with
a federal investigation?"*

"Alex, help me, I don't know what to tell them."

"I'm sorry babe, I was out back."

"Huh?"

"Come with us, Mrs. Foster."

*I followed the agent to a secret back door. When it
opened, they pushed me out in sheer laughter. I looked up at
them donned in black suits as Alex reached out for me and
said, "Shanelle, tell Willie James I said hi!"*

My body quickly jumped up from the bed as Alex
jumped out of his skin. I pulled the sheet off me and ran to
the bathroom. It was a much needed relief because I almost
released myself on the bed. Alex stood at the doorway

wiping his eyes. "Is something wrong with the baby?"

"No, I had a bad dream and I'm hungry." My body was trembling as the jolt of bright lights forced me to squint my eyes. I regretted that remark. Alex looked at me with a stern look on his face and said, "Well, I'm making something healthy for you, I talked to my mother on my way home."

"Oh," I replied. I thought they were going to keep my secret but I was wrong. "They sure do stick together," I thought.

We walked into the kitchen as Alex began to cut up watermelon and yogurt. He prepared one cupful and put it on the table with a spoon and napkin.

"Are you worried about tomorrow?" Alex asked.

"A little, why?"

"You're eating that's why."

"Well, I am pregnant Alex."

"I know, but that shouldn't be an excuse to eat this late at night."

I picked up my spoon and put the creamy substance in my mouth as it slowly went down. Alex stood up and kissed me on my forehead.

"I'm going to bed, don't stay up too late, we have a busy day tomorrow."

I watched him walk back into the bedroom and slowly close the door. The spoon in my hand clanged on the table as I laid it down. The yogurt and fruit mixed together didn't have the appeal I needed. There was no way I could do it the way I really wanted to so I had to resist. Thoughts of Alex leaving me again to go back to Philly worried me as I stood at the sink and washed my spoon off. I watered a few plants and dried the sink with a paper towel. A few magazines left over from the previous month needed to be thrown away. I dusted off the TV and adjusted the painting by the doorway until sleepiness set in. No overwhelming need to binge overcame me as I returned to the bedroom and curled up under Alex. A good night sleep came at last.

Interrogation

I was expecting Alex to take me to a large white building with tinted black glass. Instead, he drove straight to Newark and parked in an abandoned factory on Frelinghuysen Avenue.

"Why are we stopping here?" I asked.

"This is it Shanelle, they have a facility here."

I grabbed his hand as we got out the car. Alex knocked on a rustic metal door three times as a man opened the door to let us in. Alex flashed his badge as the agent in black held the door for us. A freight elevator took us up three flights to a fully modern office. I knew I was in serious trouble just by the technology in the room. Agents in black and navy single-breasted suits shuffled down the narrow hallway with paperbound books and files in their hands. Women in short skirts with guns on their hips strutted past me like they meant business. I squeezed Alex's hand in sheer nervousness as he placed his arm around my waist to comfort me. Alex greeted a few people along the way, but he never smiled. A large conference room faced us at the end of the passageway. When we entered, twelve agents stood up to greet us. A buffed agent greeted us first. He shook Alex's hand and barely looked at me as he directed us to two chairs.

"Have a seat Alex, thanks for coming on time with your wife."

Alex cleared his throat and adjusted his tie. "No problem," he said. "We just want to get this over with."

Alex's answer prompted all the agents to sit up and

pay attention as they began to pick up their pens. The agent turned to me and said, "Shanelle, I'm Special Agent Russo from the Narcotics Warrant Squad. With me today are various agents from the bureau and its surrounding agencies. We called you in today because your husband's vehicle showed up on our photograph evidence list, including photographs of you talking to our lead suspect in this investigation."

I looked at Alex for support. He patted the top of my hand as I surveyed the room of agents.

Agent Russo continued. "Shanelle, we only have a few questions for you, but we do know that your husband cannot be included in our undercover sting because of your association with the Garvey Projects and your brother Steven."

Agent Russo's surprise message caused Alex to slip his hand away and fold them in his lap. I turned to Alex to apologize, but he looked the other way. Other agents held their heads down as they paid homage to the emotionally injured officer. "Your husband has a great career in front of him, but our main concern is everyone's safety and protection during this sensitive operation."

My lips grimaced slightly as I stared at Agent Russo. He handed me a large envelope and said, "Take a look at the photographs and tell me what you know about the individuals you were seen with."

Alex sat up straight and cleared his throat as I tried to concentrate. The first photo was Mookie's mother. I smiled slightly and said, "That's Mama Barb, she takes care of everybody, especially the kids."

One of the older agents to the far left of me threw his head back and said, "Yeah, that's a good one." The other agents started laughing as if they were all in on the secret. Alex began to tap his foot and tap his finger on the table. I held my lips together as I slid another photograph from underneath the pile. It was a photo of me and Rico. I spoke over the fading laughter and replied, "That's Rico, his sister and I went to high school together."

Agent Russo leaned into me and said, "Is that all you know?" Alex went on the defensive and said, "Yeah, that's all she knows, she doesn't live there, didn't grow up there and she had no business being there." He stood up and adjusted his suit jacket as he grabbed my elbow to leave. Agent Russo stood up and motioned his hand in the air for Alex to wait.

"Just one more thing Mrs. Foster," Agent Russo said. "We have strong reason to believe that a urban bounty is on your brother's head for some expensive weapons that he allegedly stole. Your husband was smart enough to warn you once. Take his advice and stay away from the Garvey Projects."

Alex turned his back on me and headed towards the double door. Most of the agents flashed a condescending smile as I held my head down low and followed Alex. Agent Russo held the door open and said, "Alex, Captain Fisco said to report to work at your regular time tomorrow." As the large door closed behind us, there was distant laughter from the conference room. The look on Alex's face suggested that he was convinced they were laughing at him. Once outside, Alex loosened his tie and snatched it off. He walked past the car and threw his tie in the air in complete disgust. I walked a few paces behind him not realizing that he wanted to vent as my shoe slipped in a small pot hole filled with rocks. I began to brush off the side of my shoe as Alex turned around in anger.

"So that's what's important right now, you're pretty shoes Shanelle?"

"No, I slipped…"

"Damn Shanelle, I told you not to go there! Shit just keeps following you everywhere and you don't listen! You don't think either."

My heart started to beat rapidly as my body began to shrink. The voices got smart with him. The Big One said, *"Last time I checked, didn't he kill somebody?"* The Little One replied, *"Lay low Shanelle, that tie is starting to look like a noose."*

Anxiety started to kick in as I looked in multiple directions. The need to run was there, but I felt like I was in a barren wasteland. Alex started heading to the car and said, "Let's go." He opened the door for me, but when I got settled with my seatbelt, he slammed the door like a drunken fool. I followed him with my eyes as he walked around the front of the car and got in. His massive frame seemed to grow inside the car as I envisioned hot vapors steaming from his mouth and ears. His breathing got deeper as he placed his hand on my head rest and turned his head to back up the vehicle. It never required so much effort, but I swear when he put his hands back on the steering wheel, he looked like he wanted to smack me in my face. Instead he just looked at me and rolled his eyes. I was immobile and two inches short of sheer terror. Alex sped down Frelinghuysen and then to Broad Street in five minutes flat. We passed Zanzibar and headed for the New Jersey Turnpike. Alex snatched the Turnpike ticket and shifted the gears in one swift motion. The need to let it out engulfed into a screaming match.

"I asked you to do one thing Shanelle, one thing and you didn't listen to me. I ask my mother to do something and she does it. Any of my sisters, they do it. Here it is my wife, just short of one week married, baby on the way eating a two piece in the projects with the lead suspect in an undercover operation that I was lucky enough to get assigned to! Now, because of you, I'm back on the beat in a boring ticket assignment just because you feel like acting like a project girl!"

Exhaustion began to set in as I reclined my seat back and processed the rest of Alex's rage. His Mazda felt like the closet Steven and I shared in Steven's fits of psychosis. His voice sounded like a wild night with Mrs. Viv, after a hard days work, with the sudden surprise of dirty dishes in the sink. I turned to the side silently numb and faced the passenger window as Alex weaved in and out of traffic.

I closed my eyes and said, "They're nice people Alex, I didn't think I was doing any harm by going there." I yawned again and threw his precious seedling in his face. "Besides, all this yelling is not good for the baby."

My good guess was right. He turned on the radio and began to slow down as he shifted his gear down a notch. The engine raced a brief moment and settled down as Alex adjusted the station to CD 101.9. Defeated and exhausted, I slept the rest of the way home under the cloak of Alex's second rage.

Silent Treatment

Back at the apartment, the silence between us was deafening as Alex quickly made phone calls to his family. He spoke to his father first; slumped in the couch like he lost his best friend. I took a quick bath and climbed into bed for a nap. I could barely hear what Alex was saying but at least he wasn't venting on me. It was enough embarrassment and shame for one day and I didn't want to hear anymore about it. Neither one of us had dinner that night. Even though he was home, he chose to sleep on the couch. I wanted him to wrap me up in his arms, but he wouldn't come near me. The next morning, Alex quietly slipped in the bedroom and took his uniform and underwear out of the closet. I pretended to sleep as I focused on my aching heart. It felt like it was burning on the inside as my head began to tingle. Alex tiptoed around the room until it was time to leave. I could hear a few dishes clanging in the sink and smelled toast and bacon. I was too ashamed to get up and join him for breakfast, so I continued to lay there. Keys began to jingle in the distance. The bedroom door opened as Alex walked up to me. He sat on the bed and softly stroked my hair. My longing for him forced my eyes open. I hoped to see forgiveness in his eyes but instead it was extreme sadness.

"Good morning," he said as he stroked my hairline. "I'm leaving for work. I left your breakfast in the oven and cut up some oranges for you." I grabbed his wrist as I continued to lay there. I didn't want to cry, but it was coming.

In a soft pitiful moan I said, "I'm so sorry Alex."

Alex kissed my forehead and replied. "I know baby. I love you and I'll see you later." I held on to his wrist as he pulled away from me and headed to the door.

The pain of Alex leaving me was too much to bare. The sheets fell to the floor as I headed for the kitchen. In addition to the breakfast in the oven, I finished off the cream cheese and a cupful of peanut butter. The sound of the phone ringing instantly interrupted my frenzy. I looked at the phone after the third ring and contemplated ignoring the call. But after the damage I caused, it would have been a foolish move. I forced the rest of the food down my throat and answered. "Hello."

"Shanelle, hi baby, it's me, mama.

The tone in here voice took me back to childhood as I sat down on the kitchen chair. I wiped the residue from around my mouth and replied, "Hi mama, how are you, how is everything?"

"Fine Shanelle, I called to see how you were feeling?"

The soft compassion in her voice forced tears to my eyes as the eggs and bacon swelled in my throat. "I did a stupid thing mama." There was compassion in her voice as she asked, "What happened Shanelle?"

I wanted to tell her, but the bouts of isolation between the two of us could not compel my answer. I loved her, but I wasn't willing to risk more negative judgments. Besides, the news would only hurt her more. Most of it was about Steven's thievery sprees at Garvey. I wanted her to be safe, so it was best for me to leave it alone. I asked, "How's daddy, I miss him so much."

She breathed a sigh of relief and replied, "We both miss you sweetheart, he was so excited when I told him I saw you at Shoprite. He wants you to come visit him Shanelle." My leg started to bounce up and down in a nervous response.

"I'm sorry mama, I can't come to the house, maybe we could meet somewhere."

There was a long pause between us. There was also desperation in her voice. "Why can't you come home Shanelle, we love you."

Both of my legs began to bounce as I grabbed the phone cord. "Then why did you do that to me mama? Why did I always have to pack my bags and go, I didn't do anything wrong."

"Shanelle, we didn't know what to do. We were so afraid of losing Steven in the street, we did everything we could to keep him home and medicated."

Air filled my lungs and head. I felt dizzy. The answer was too much to handle. It was riddled with more confusion and doubt. Worst of all, it only meant that she loved Steven more than me. In retrospect, that kind of love led me into the streets for sanctuary. In fact, it led me straight into Alex's arms, good, bad or indifferent.

"Mama, the door bell is ringing, I have to go, I'll call you later." I didn't wait for her to respond as I hung up. There was no one at the door, but at least there was silence. I immediately thought of Tammy. With nowhere to go, all I could do was to stay busy. I took out a pad and paper and made a list of things to do. Clean up, take a shower and write a letter to mom and dad. The letter came first.

Dear mom and dad:

After all that's happened, I can still honestly say that I love you both. I want to hate you, but I can't. It's a strange paradox feeling this way, but I struggle with it every day. You missed an important time in my life so it's hard for me to tell you what's new in my life. Everything is not so peachy keen because of the emptiness that comes from not having you in my life. We've got some wounds to heal and that's going to take time. In the meantime, we're expecting our first baby on April 27th. The Fosters are my in-laws and have been very good to me. I'm trying to be a good wife and continue school. I haven't forgotten my dreams and maybe one day they'll come true. It's hard for me to say when I'll see you again. I resume classes at St. James in the fall and I have a full course schedule. Maybe we can meet in the fall when I'm on that side of town. Other than that, life is going in any direction the wind takes me.

Love Always,

Shanelle

I sealed the letter and quietly put it in an envelope. I looked around and decided that instead of binging, I was going to clean the apartment. Working on each room at a time, I dusted, swept and polished each room to a bright and shiny finish. I marinated chicken and took out string beans for steaming. A few citrus candles enhanced the aroma in the apartment. The TV remote needed to be where Alex left it last. For his own comfort and convenience, I needed to stay out of his way in case he was still angry at me.

I took a long shower and washed my hair. My preparation for him needed to be perfect, yet understated. A touch of Safari perfume tapped my hips and shoulder blades. An ankle length sheer gown complimented my naked frame. The pouch in my stomach was just the right touch since he loved to talk to my belly. While dinner slowly simmered, I quickly changed the sheets on the bed and fluffed up the pillows. The voices giggled behind my back in doubt.

"She sure is making a fuss for him tonight." The

sound of Alex's key in the door and a quick look at the clock was my cue to greet him at the foyer. He walked through the door and immediately looked around. He smiled at me briefly and walked past me as my arms slumped from his immediate rejection.

"Smells good Shanelle, what did you cook?" My nerves followed me to the kitchen as I leaned against the counter. "Oh, grilled chicken and steamed vegetables." The sight of me barely fazed him as he walked past and went into the bedroom. Before he went inside, he threw his hat and badge on the coffee table. After that the door slammed.

"Hmph," the Little One said. *"All that cleaning for nothing, you're so stupid Shanelle."* My fingernail slowly tapped on the kitchen table as I contemplated my next move. The silence was killing me and there was nothing left for me to do except fix his plate. I didn't know how hungry he was so I made a small portion. Five minutes past and there was no sound from the room. I sat at the table and put my head in my hand as my elbow rested on the table. Suddenly Alex emerged, barefoot and wearing white cotton boxers. His skin was smooth as silk as I watched him grab the remote and plop on the couch. Silence rested between us as the TV became our buffer. Suddenly, the phone rang. When Alex answered he stared at the earpiece and then hung up.

"Wrong number?" I asked.

He held the remote to the TV and said, "Whoever it was hung up."

"Oh." I replied. I wondered if it was Steven. If it was, now wasn't the time to bring him up. "Are you hungry Alex?"

"Yeah, gimme a minute Shanelle, I'm tired." I quickly made his plate and sat it on the table. His fork and knife were lined up perfectly next to his favorite plate. Three cubes of ices clanging in his favorite glass brought back a faint memory of the day I saw him at the wedding. He was so graceful and handsome that day, I would have given anything to turn back the clock and do it right this time. I looked down at my stomach and then at Alex. His head was resting in the fold of his arm as he listened to the news. All I wanted to do was eat something fast and furious but there was no way I could do that now. I walked into the bedroom and climbed into bed, hurt and defeated. Alex picked up the phone and hung it up. In five minutes the phone rang.

"Hey Jack, what's up dog?"

"Nah. I'm cool, Captain Fisco said he was going to make a few calls and see if I can get another assignment, but in a way I'm glad because I need to be closer to Shanelle."

I slid my body across the bed towards the edge and continued to listen.

"Nah man, you know I can't be mad at her too long, I'm crazy about her." He laughed a little at Jack's response and said, "Watch your mouth man, that's my wife when you get finished. We'll work it out, but listen, I just saw point man on the news. They just bumped him up to maximum security. They said a few leaks got back to the runners and blew their cover down on Runyon in Newark. Yeah man, no kidding. Even if they put me on, we won't be together anyway."

I didn't have any clue what Alex was talking about, but whatever information he shared with Jack seemed important.

"Listen, come by this weekend and bring your new girlfriend, we can grill on the patio. What was your score at the range?" Alex started laughing and said, "Not bad, not bad. Ok, I'll see you Saturday."

Instead of climbing under the covers, I put the sheet over my hips. My eyes began to close as I listened to Alex's fork hit his plate. He never asked me to join him so I stayed in the room. Sleep became me so fast I was glad I had the escape. I don't know how long I slept, but when I rolled over he was stroking my hips with his fingertips. His face was an inch within mine staring quietly at my stomach. He startled me at first, but it settled just by the warmth of his touch. Alex began to stroke my face and lips with his thumb. I searched his eyes for questions, doubts or simple rhetoric, but I couldn't read him. Alex buried his head in my neck and took a deep breath. I held him back as my body began to shiver in his arms. Alex ran his hand up and down my back until I began to moan. The power of his touch was all I needed for his forgiveness. He slid down and rested his head against my stomach and began to kiss my belly button. "Hey Pumpy, I bet it's nice and warm in there." I started to giggle as my stomach heaved up and down. He palmed my stomach with his hand and said, "You look so sexy pregnant Shanelle."

I didn't care what I looked like. I was happy that he was talking to me again. Even if he needed space, it hurt like hell, but at least he was craving and touching me again. I draped my leg on his back as an invitation to love me in anyway imaginable. In Alex's world, the only thing that seemed to calm him was caressing my stomach. He placed his head closer to my womb and quietly fell asleep as I stroked his smooth hair into my own surrender. It wasn't long before another dream haunted me.

A quick poke to the back of my head complimented his greeting. "Hey fatso, tough game tonight huh?"

"Leave me alone."

"Your thighs can't get you up that court fast enough you fake point guard. You're really a line backer you know."

"Shut up Steven."

A cool steel blade pierced my notebook as he grabbed my neck. "Let me borrow ten dollars fatty."

"No! Get off of me."

The rise of my arm forced his defense as he twisted it behind my back. "Get in the closet stupid, they're coming."

The door slammed and the phobias set in.

"Let me out!"

He started laughing as the sound of keys and coins fell from my pocket book as he searched every crevice.

"Oh yeah, hiding a twenty from me fatty? Who gave you this money, that bitch ass around the corner? I saw the way you kissed him on Stirling Avenue slut, mommy's gonna beat your ass when I tell her."

"No, don't tell please!"

The door opened and he came inside. His hot funky breath rested on my face as he shamed my existence. "I better not hear my little sister is sleeping around or I'll cut your ass you hear me?"

The closet started to spin in a violent circle as he mushed my head to the floor. "Don't come out until you hear the front door close fatty."

The creaking steps supported his demonic existence as he left the house. My steps followed in tow as his evil intentions filled my brain straight to the kitchen. The note on the refrigerator seemed to stand out like a six foot poster. "Shanelle, cook pork chops tonight with peas, make sure Steven takes his medicine and don't fight. If I find out you've been fighting, I'm going to beat your ass."

Comfort rested in three scoops of peanut butter, four donuts and Dannon yogurt. Steven returned unannounced through the back door. "See, that's why you're so fat bitch. Put that peanut butter back before I tell mom." The shame and fear of it all forced me to surrender. Steven grabbed a soiled paper bag off the counter top and slithered through the back door like a thief in broad daylight. Heavy breathing kicked in as I stocked the shelves back and hummed my own tune to God. "Yes, Jesus loves me, yes

Jesus loves me, yes Jesus loves me 'cause the bible tells me so." I looked up and said, "Even though I'm doing right by You, this sure doesn't feel right."

Suddenly I realized I was dreaming. My clothes were so drenched I needed to change. Alex was sleeping so heavy he never felt me wake up. I went to the bathroom and contemplated eating, but I was too drained from the dream. Instead I made some tea and rolled up on the couch with a comforter. The remote became my friend into the early morning as I watched the Dukes of Hazzards and thought, "Damn that Daisy, she's so skinny."

Accepting Change

By the time November rolled around, there was enough family and holiday excitement to keep me busy. Candy finally came home after staying an extra month in Pittsburg. She hooked up with Tammy and Nicole one time as a courtesy to me, but I knew Candy wasn't feeling my sister-in-law. Candy got a job as a flight attendant for Continental Airlines. Miss Thang traveled domestic and international flights four times a week and had the weekends off. She brought me souvenirs from all around the world including cute flowing tops to compliment my shape. We barely had time to spend together, so we made a point of hooking up on Fridays before I headed back to Lakewood. Every time she saw me she kissed my belly like a happy fool. She was excited about being a Godmother, but she was hell bent on not changing pampers.

Pumpy was growing by leaps and bounds. An ultrasound confirmed two months ago that Alex and I were having a boy. My face and stomach was as round as Florence from Good Times. The entire Foster family agreed that being pregnant with a baby boy made a woman beautiful and they were right. My skin was flawless and my hair grew past my shoulders. There was nothing but dreamy looks every time Alex stared at me. There was so much happiness around me, change came with the comfort of knowing people loved me without ridicule and judgment. I decided that my world needed to stay that way, especially for my baby. The slightest negativity from anyone sent me into avoidance, so I simply wrapped myself up in the warmth of people who truly cared about me.

My classes were intellectually stimulating. I learned so much about myself and my ability to voice opinion about the world around me. I usually spent an extra ten minutes chatting with my professors about international politics and children's rights. Several professors encouraged me to seek an internship in Washington next year to see congress in action. I considered the thought by writing in my journal: *"Washington; a dream deferred for now."* In the meantime, the health and safety of my unborn child consumed my thoughts as I put my future career on hold.

I had small bouts of sadness at St. James because there weren't too many people interested in hanging out with the "prego girl" Ring or not, I didn't look fashionable next to any girl trying to make a name for herself. On sadder days, I watched girls my age hustle by in cute jeans and tops, holding hands with their college beaus. There was intellectual and social divide for me on a daily basis. It wasn't like I could hang out at the pubs with beer and cigarettes in my hand; it wasn't healthy for me or Pumpy. I met a few older women in my classes who rallied around my progress. I encouraged their youthful exuberance and they encouraged me to accept the things I could not change for now. Overall, I was glad to have Candy in my life because she was down with me no matter what.

As for Alex, he seemed to slowly forgive me after the Garvey thing. He settled back into his routine simply because I did the things that made him happy. That was his definition in our relationship. After several sleepless nights, I figured out that Alex loved me, but there was another side to him that didn't sit right with me. I only saw it twice, but I never wanted to see it again. My resolve was that acceptance to change made him a happy man. As long as he believed that I was conducting myself like a lady and being a good mother to his son, there was no need for him to act like a raging beast. Like some unwritten code of conduct, I was a loyal wife and he was a good husband. We respected each other's boundaries, but Alex defined my limits without any input from me. Alex defined his own code of conduct in our marriage. To the outside world, he looked absolutely perfect. It was a strange dynamic, but it beat the cruel abyss I left so long ago.

In preparation for finals, I stayed at Candy's house Tuesday through Friday and came home after hooking up with Candy. Alex brought me a used four door Toyota Camry to get back and forth. He had full confidence in me again in my decision not to return home or to Garvey. I called him from Candy's house every night before I went to bed. It was hard not being with him, but he knew how much an education at St. James University meant to me. One week shy of Thanksgiving, I stayed late at the library studying. The campus was fluttering with activity as students and faculty prepared for homecoming festivities. At five months, Pumpy was an active baby inside my womb, but usually settled in after seven p.m. My hands were glued to my belly all the time. There was nothing left to do but fixate on my growing stomach. It was a miracle of our love and I was growing fond of motherhood as the days went by.

Bonnie was at Morgan State University raising hell and selling jewelry to get by. She was still kickin' it with her grammar school sweet heart and she called every now and then to say hi. Memories of all my friends filled my face with a soft smile as I sat at the table. I picked up my pen to jot down a few notes, when suddenly, an old friend walked up to the table and placed a biology book next to me. I looked up with complete astonishment.

"Shanelle?"

"Derrick?"

I followed his handsome face as he walked around

the table next to me. I immediately stood up to hug him. Derrick leaned in to me carefully as if I were a delicate swan. He rubbed my back with small circles and said, "It's so good to see you, look at you." Derrick grabbed my left hand and studied my ring finger. "Married too no doubt, my how time flies, who's the lucky guy?" He was still as charming as ever. He placed his hands behind his back and tapped his foot while he waited for an answer. I folded my hands across my stomach and said, "Alex Foster, he's a police officer."

Derrick shook his head up and down and placed his hand under his chin in heavy thought.

"Ah yes," He replied, "Honor, serve and protect."

I began to rub my belly as I chuckled at his response, "Yes, you can say that." I wanted to know more about him so I tapped his arm and said, "So, what's been up with you after all this time Dr. Johnson?"

He was beaming with pride and said, "First year medical student, Gross Anatomy, merit scholar, little bit of this, little bit of that."

I egged him on by tapping his arm. "And, how's your love life?"

He began to rock back and forth and said, "No one special, I was hoping you would still be around." His almond shaped eyes and warm smile melted my entire frame. I didn't feel anything for him, but he made me feel special.

"Enough about me Shanelle, how are you feeling, look at you, you're beautiful."

I held my head down, but he picked it back up. "Keep your head up lady, there's nothing down there except feet and shoes." He leaned into me and whispered, "I'm sorry, maybe you can't see your shoes." Like old times, I smacked his arm and said, "Shut up Derrick!" He grabbed my hand and said, "You know I'm just playing Shanelle."

Derrick looked around at the patrons staring at us and softly whispered, "Do you want to go to the sub shop for coffee, uh, well maybe milk and cookies?"

I giggled like a little kid and said, "Sure, I would love that."

Like the days gone by, in an innocent gesture, Derrick picked up my books and escorted me out the library. There was a chill in the air so he stopped and waited for me to button up my swing coat.

"Nice and warm now?" He asked.

"Yes, I'm fine," I said, as my face blushed over like the good ole days. Crisp leaves in red, yellow and brown swept by us as we walked across the campus. Derrick carefully slowed down his pace. He looked down at me and said, "You look so cute waddling like a little mama duck."

I put my hand through his arm and said, "You know you're the only person who can get away with a comment like that."

He patted my hand like an old acquaintance and said, "I know Shanelle, I know."

We walked past the black iron gates of the University as I pointed out my car. "Hey let's put my books in the car so you don't have to carry them."

Derrick looked down at me and said, "It's no bother Shanelle, I'll carry your books anytime."

I felt like a teenager all over again as I continued to hold onto his arm. "Still the gentleman Derrick."

"Always a gentleman Shanelle."

Derrick escorted me to a booth in the back of the Campus Sub Shop. He helped me out of my coat and held my arm as I sat in the booth. I smoothed out my clothes and crossed my ankles as Derrick went to the counter and ordered two caffeine free hot chocolates with whipped cream. His side profile was absolutely dashing and I was sure he found some new hair care products to tame his wild wooly hair. His new mustache made him look more mature as he waited to pay the cashier. A few guys came in the store and gave him his proffers. "Yo D, what's up, how's life at Cornell Med?" Derrick rhythmically shook hands and pounded chests with them as they looked up to the mighty alumni. He turned to look at me and smiled as I our eyes met.

"It's going well, thanks," he said, as he walked away. Derrick slid into the booth and passed the steaming cup towards me.

"Be careful, it's really hot."

I couldn't resist and said, "Like I used to be?"

Derrick leaned into the table and said, "Girl, you're still hot, Alex is a lucky guy."

I looked down at my bulging belly and said, "Yeah he is lucky."

Derrick looked at me and said, "Are you happy Shanelle, you've been through so much?"

I sighed and said, "Sometimes I'm happy and sometimes I'm just relieved that all of that is behind me."

"What about you Derrick, are you happy?" I asked.

Derrick leaned back into his booth and took a deep breath. "Academically yes, my life is on the fast track. I just haven't found my soul mate and I really want that Shanelle." He cleared his throat and said, "Remember all the plans we used to have?"

"Yes," I replied.

"Well it takes a lot to juggle your time and attention between medical school and trying to nurture a relationship. I barely have time for myself." He paused and then said, "Some of these girls out here are not hearing it Shanelle. They're not willing to put their lives on hold while I waste away in a library."

I sipped my hot chocolate and said, "Hmm, sounds like someone I know."

Derrick took a sip of his hot chocolate and said, "I think if I stayed local I could have convinced you Shanelle."

I looked at my watch and said, "We'll never know Derrick."

He shook his head up and down and said, "You're right."

"Hey, whatever happened to Portia?" I asked.

Derrick's face got really serious. "Bad news, Ricky called me and told me that she left Spelman. He said she went to a frat party and things got out of hand. Portia cried rape and her father went storming down there with a pocket full of money and expensive attorneys. I'm not going to mention the university, but two leading scorers were expelled after the indictment. You know her father had to get her out of there. She was getting death threats from all across the country for messing up the point spread the night of the incident. You know basketball is big business down there. I heard she's laying low taking classes right here at St. James."

"Really, I haven't seen her at all."

"She probably doesn't want to be seen."

"How's your mother Derrick?"

"Good," Derrick replied. "She asks about you all the time."

"Oh, that's nice, tell her I said hello." I looked at my watch just like long ago and said, "Listen, I better run, it's getting late."

"Where do you live Shanelle?" Derrick asked.

"I live in Lakewood, but I stay at Candy's house during the week."

"Oh," Derrick replied.

I slid from out of the booth and said, "Derrick, it was really good seeing you again. Thanks for the hot chocolate."

Derrick grabbed my hand and said, "It was really good seeing you again too Shanelle." He helped me put my coat on again and nodded to the guys behind him.

Even though we said our goodbyes at the sub shop, Derrick walked me to my car and watched me pull off. I looked through the rear view mirror and whispered, "It was really good seeing him again."

By the time I got home, Candy's father Leonard had already retired for the night. He left a note on the table that read, *Page Candy, she has a layover in D.C. and call Alex now, he called three times."*

I looked at my watch. It was already nine thirty and I knew he was worried about me. When I dialed home, he picked up on the first ring.

"Shanelle?"

"Hi baby."

"Why are you getting in so late, I was worried."

"Oh, I stayed at the library to cram for finals, but I'm okay."

"How's my son?"

"He's fine as always Alex. I love you."

"I love you too, I wish you were home."

"Alex, I have finals and I need to study."

Alex sighed and said, I know, I'll see you tomorrow after work."

"Ok."

"Goodnight mommy."

"Goodnight Alex."

As I walked up the stairs I began to surrender again. The need in his voice led me straight down the stairs and to the telephone. I dialed the number and exhaled.

"Hello."

I cleared my throat and said, "It's me honey."

"I know, what's up?"

"I think I'm going to transfer to Monmouth University. Don't get me wrong, I love St. James, but I want to be closer to you."

Alex breathed a sigh of relief and said, "Sounds good to me, I'll call tomorrow and request an application."

I went to the blue room and climbed into bed for a restful sleep. I was longing for Alex's touch, but I knew that it wouldn't be long before I saw him.

The next day I met Candy for an early dinner. She was exhausted, but wanted to see me just the same. She handed me a gift bag with two outfits for her Godson.

"Candy, stop buying everything and wait until he gets here."

"Girl, stop telling me what I can and cannot buy. You know I'm going to spoil him and when I have my own, you better spoil mine rotten too."

She looked at my face and said, "You look happy, what's new?"

I ordered a Greek salad and handed the waitress the menu. "No big surprises girl, I'm just trying to make sense of everything and taking charge. You know, the baby, classes and Alex."

"Alex is your toughest challenge I bet," Candy replied.

"Yeah he is, but we'll work it out as long as he gives me a little space. He is trying Candy." I paused and said, "Oh yeah, I'm going to take two classes in the spring just to get ready for the baby and transfer to Monmouth University."

"Well, that's good, but you know we won't see each other as much. I'm getting ready to do Newark to L.A. three times a week to cut down on my fatigue. The money is nice, but girl I'm tired. Clinton and I are getting more and more serious and it's hard keeping up with his sexy ass."

"Do you love him Candy?" I asked.

Candy rolled her eyes around in her head as she sipped her diet ice tea. "Oh Shanelle," Candy exhaled, "You are such a sucker for romance. But yes, since you asked, we are in love."

I grabbed her hand and said, "Please have a big wedding but wait till Pumpy is born so he can be in it with us."

"Oh, now you're planning my wedding?"

"Well you were trying to plan mine! Just give me the date and I'm there girl."

We toasted our glasses and ate our meal over chatty small talk. Candy looked so pretty being in love and I was genuinely happy for her. Parts of me wanted to hop on the next flight and hang out with her, but I could sense she wanted to slow up her pace too. We walked to the parking lot together and Candy gave my belly a good rub before she hugged me goodbye. To her surprise, Pumpy gave her a swift kick. She smiled at me and said, "Shanelle, did you feel that, my Godson kicked me?" I laughed out loud and said, "Of course I did silly. Let me get on the parkway girl, I'll call you later." Candy hopped in her Miata and said, "Ok, I love you girl."

By the time I got home it was just getting dark outside. Alex greeted me at the door and took my overnight bag and books. He kissed me on the forehead and said, "Dinner's ready if you're hungry." At a quick glance, it looked like Alex cleaned the entire apartment.

I looked at him and said, "Actually, I want to take a bath first."

Alex carried my bag to the laundry room area and said, "I'll run some water, can I join you?"

"Sure," I replied.

The bathroom was fresh and clean just the way I liked it. Alex began to run the water as I peeled out of my black tights and maternity dress. He turned around as he tested the water with a smile on his face. "You look beautiful Shanelle." Parts of me began to feel beautiful but it was hard. My breasts were full and erect and my stomach was round and hard. Alex stared at me like a Scooby Snack as I slipped into the warm water. He quickly followed as I moved forward to make room for him. Laying back into his chest was like slow motion relief. Alex held his hands up and let small droplets of water drip on my breasts as I closed my eyes. He stroked my inner thighs up and down as my head rolled to the other side. His deep voice sounded like a Barry melody as he whispered in my ear, "I'm proud of you baby." My lips barely moved as I enjoyed the splendor of his touch. "Proud of what?" Alex rubbed soap into his hands and ran his fingers up and down my neck with gentle pressure.

"Well," Alex said. "I used to worry about you all the time; especially the eating thing."

I opened my eyes momentarily and said, "I know, I'm trying to stay focused. Tammy helped a lot too. Besides, as long as there's no pressure in my life to do and be all these things, I think I can manage." I twirled my hand through the milky water as I contemplated another confession. "It's hard talking about it Alex even though I know you wont judge me. I kept things from my family so they wouldn't judge or criticize me and I'm trying to find a way to open up more to you."

"Just take your time baby, it will come," Alex said.

"Sometimes I get so worked up when I'm stressed, that I feel like I have a million voices in my head."

Alex spread his fingers throughout the back of my scalp and said, "Maybe you are your toughest critic Shanelle. Just take it one day at a time."

Missing him the way I did, I grabbed Alex's hands and pushed them under my breasts. The sheer size of them filled his big hands as he used his thumbs to stroke my nipples.

"I missed you Alex."

"Me too," Alex replied.

Alex turned the hot water on again as I shifted my body weight to the side. The pregnancy made it difficult for me to manipulate myself in the tub, but I managed to turn. Alex caressed my face and kissed me long and hard as he called my name in between kisses. The feeling was just the right touch before a quiet dinner.

Safety came first so Alex got out of the tub first and wrapped himself up in a towel. He handed me a towel and held me by the hand like I was a precious package. He wrapped me up and then got enticed about what was underneath. I went into the bedroom and picked out a white sheer gown that fell just past my behind. It was his favorite piece because it gave him easy access. A pair of matching sheer panties gave it just the right touch. Alex walked up behind me and nuzzled my neck. "Let's eat," he said, as he swept his hands under my panties. My nipples became so hard he walk around me and sat me on the edge of the bed. Alex knelt down and talked to my stomach. My eyes rolled back in my head as Alex laid me down and put his face between my legs. He bit Kitty right through my panties as I held his head in pure delight. The sheer fabric and his thick tongue was just the right touch as I began to swell in his mouth. He slid my panties off and finished me off while he massaged my thighs. My legs slumped to the floor in pure fatigue.

Alex stood up and went to the bathroom for a quick gargle. By the time he came back, I was under the covers trying to sleep. He peeled the covers back and said, "Not yet, I'm not finished and you need to eat." He slid behind me and kissed the small of my back. "C'mon Shanelle," Alex said, "Get up." I rolled over and rested my head under his chin. I pleaded with him to let me sleep but he wouldn't let me. "You're too sexy to sleep right now and besides, I want to make love to you."

Alex picked up my robe and helped me put it on. We

sat on the patio and ate dinner under the stars. Alex picked my feet up and rested it on his legs while we ate steam vegetables and shrimp. I noticed him watching me and said, "What, tell me."

He caressed my chin with his hand and said, "I'm a lucky man Shanelle."

I put my plate on my lap and said, "So what makes you so lucky?" It didn't take much for him to answer.

"You came into my life and accepted me for me Shanelle. I know things have been a little crazy for us, but you are one tough cookie. Then there are parts of you that remind me of the sweetest chocolate melting in my mouth." Alex took my plate and put it on the table. He grabbed my hand and led me into the living room as he dimmed the lights. Alex pulled me to the middle of the floor and began to dance with me. The quiet still of the evening and the open patio doors was just the right touch as I began to shake off the sleepies.

"Remember the night we met again at the wedding?" He asked.

"Yes," I replied, "I remember."

Alex held my hand against his chest and said, "You looked like the sweetest angel in pink when I realized it was you."

I giggled in the dark as my big belly pressed into his flat stomach. "Actually, I was wearing fuscia." Alex laughed in my ear in the sexiest way and said, "You're right, I stand corrected." He pulled me in closer to him and said, "I remember when you got up and walked out. I thought you were leaving so I followed you to make sure you didn't leave me again."

"Oh?"

"My palms were so sweaty, I had to wipe it on my tux."

"Yes, that beautiful Armani tux, you were so handsome."

He chuckled and said, "I still got it going on girl."

I slid my hands down the back of his boxers and said, "You might say that officer."

The clock alarm kicked in as Vaughn Harper's silky voice emitted through the speakers. He played Very Special by Debra Laws as we danced in our bare feet.

"We better enjoy this now," Alex said. "When Pumpy gets here, we'll be too tired."

The laughter in my voice was light and sweet. "We'll put him between us that's all." Alex sang the entire song to me as he stroked my back and breasts. He was so smooth he danced me back to the bedroom and on to the bed. He couldn't pick me up like the old days. I was finally too heavy for him to sweep me off my feet. Making love at five months became a chore too, but Alex was good at taking his time. In fact, creative foreplay was his specialty. I bit my lip as he laid me on my side and entered me. It was the easy way to make love without Pumpy getting in the way. Alex bit my neck and stroked my nipples into hard rocks. My stomach tensed up as Kitty grooved to the swell of Alex's entry. Alex put his finger in my mouth as I sucked them with pure delight. He held my hip down with his hand to intensify his pleasure as he bit my neck. Good thing it was cold enough for turtlenecks, because Alex put the biggest hickey on my neck and he didn't care who saw his passion mark. Alex grabbed my hand as we locked our fingers down to compliment his release into me. The pleasure he felt kept him engorged as he continue to rock his manhood into me for another five minutes. By the time he was finished, we both fell asleep in pure coital exhaustion. Alex whispered in his sleep that making love during my pregnancy was incredible. Just from the look on his face, I knew he wasn't telling a tall tale. Suddenly the phone began to ring. Both of us were too exhausted to pick it up but we managed to strain our ears as the answering machine went off in the living room.

"Hi son, uh, hi Shanelle, it's me Pops, call me when you get a minute, I have some news for you." Alex immediately jumped up and went into the living room. It was unusual for his father to call this time of night so Alex must have sensed something was wrong. His conversation sent shock waves through my body.

"Hey Pops what's up?"

Erie silence followed.

"When?" Alex asked.

"Just you, you don't think that will look suspicious?"

"What time is your flight?"

"Ok, uh, no, I'm off tomorrow so I'll take you to the airport, no problem."

"Shanelle, she's fine, we were in the bed when you called. Ok Pops, I'll see you tomorrow at 6:00 a.m."

I sat up in bed and waited for Alex to tell me what happened. He looked like he saw a ghost and I was convinced his past finally caught up with him.

"What happened?" I asked.

Alex slid under the covers and said, "Grandma Mae, she passed away this morning."

I grabbed his hand and said, "I'm so sorry Alex."

He shook his head as I offered my sympathy and said, "She lived a good life Shanelle and she gave me a new one."

Confusion gripped my face as he stroked my cheek.

"Pops said that Grandma Mae had cement poured in the pet cemetery last month. She had a playground installed there for all of her grands and great-grands. She must have known she was leaving the earth. I'm just sorry I didn't say goodbye."

I pressed my forehead against his cheek and said,

"Alex, there's so many ways to say goodbye, just think of something and we'll do it. I don't want this to eat you up inside." Alex got off the bed and started to put his sweat pants on.

"Where are you going?" I asked.

"The beach, do you want to come?"

I was worn out and exhausted, but I didn't want him to go alone. I threw on a heavy Gap sweat suit and a baseball cap as we headed out the door. Slow tears streamed down Alex's face as we headed for the shore. I leaned my head on his arm as he quietly dealt with his grief. I didn't know what to say to him as we walked onto the sand. The cold air awakened my senses as I inhaled. Pumpy moved for a minute as I rubbed my stomach to connect with him. Alex held my hand and looked up at the sky. Tears continued to stream down his face but he remained poised.

"I looked for you in the stars Shanelle and asked God to send you to me. I also asked God to forgive me for the awful thing I did that night to protect my mother's honor. I have to fight like hell to keep the rage in me locked away in a quiet place so no harm will come to anyone who harms my family. I'd do it all over again if I had to Shanelle, and keep atoning for my sins until I die."

The wind pierced through our skin so hard that Alex had to wrap me up in our blanket as he held me. Alex continued to look at the dark waters and said, "Thank you Grandma Mae for what you did for me. I love you and I'm sorry I never had a chance to say that to you."

It was too cold to sit and reflect. Alex could feel me shivering through the blanket as he wiped his final tear away.

"C'mon, let me get you home where it's warm." I think if there was no forgiveness in the world, the cold sand would have opened up a large vacuous hole and sucked us straight to hell. I walked lightly across the sand unsure that it was going to happen like a bad nightmare from the past. I looked up at my warrior and squeezed his hand. All the things I needed were within my reach as Alex ceremoniously accepted his faults and asked for forgiveness. All the things I needed to stand on my own were questionable. I squinted my eyes as the sharp wind cut into my face. A kind voice spoke to me as I walked with Alex to the car.

"Stay by his side, forget the past, trust him and no harm will come to me in the dark of night or light of day." In some strange ceremony, when we arrived home, Alex and I washed away our past with a hot shower. We cried in each other's arms and forgave each other for the squabbles and doubts that came between us. Pumpy was our greatest joy as Alex kissed my stomach under the covers. He set the alarm for five o'clock in the morning and within an instant we were sleep.

Flashback

The sound of the phone ringing woke me up as I rolled over on Alex's side of the bed. I looked at the clock and by now he should have been home or almost home from the airport. I cleared my throat and answered.

"Hello."

"How's my little nephew Shanelle?"

"Steven, I told you not call here."

Another voice chimed in from the living room to emphasize my message.

"Yeah Steven, you heard my wife, she told you not to call here, do I need to come over there and remind you?"

A dial tone followed Alex's message as I hunched down under the covers. I didn't realize he was home and I was scared that the past we buried last night came right back. Alex walked through the bedroom door and stared at me. I immediately confessed unsure what he was going to do.

"I'm sorry Alex, he only called here once. He stole the money I gave my mother and it had our phone number written on it, uh, you were so mad at me after Garvey I never got a chance…"

Alex put his fingers to my lips and said, "Shanelle, relax, it's ok."

My chest was heaving up and down so fast Alex laid his hand on my chest to settle me down.

"Don't do this girl, I'm not mad, I just want you to be safe, that's why I flipped out about Garvey." I searched his eyes for the truth and he seemed genuine. I leaned back on the bed while Alex went to the fridge for some water.

He opened it up, handed it to me and said, "Shanelle, your brother is in the red with a lot of people. I can't say much, but he's basically a wanted crack head. I'm surprised he had the balls to call you, but whatever is going on, he must be desperate." Alex kissed me on the forehead and grabbed his car keys.

"Where are you going?" I asked.

The look on his face was distant. "I have a few errands to run, I'll be back by noon."

As Alex rolled out of the parking lot I nestled under the covers for a second nap. Intuition was the last thing on my mind as my eyes shut. Just as my world became a safer place, a blue wall of silence fell over North Orange for operation Sitting Bull. In the year that it took Alex and I to fall in love and conceive a child, I accepted everything he did without question. I was so blind, it didn't make sense to ask. Ultimately, everything happens at great sacrifice and that day, redemption fell on Garvey Street. The point man Alex referred to by phone was the infamous criminal I saw on the news months ago. He was Rico's first cousin from Garvey. Rico was second in command for Garvey, even though point man lived in the Fordham section of the Bronx. Six caseloads of glocks, five kilo's of coke and five hundred crack viles were stored in Mama Barb's apartment moving in and out under the guise of five dollar chicken dinners. Steven fucked up because he decided to take advantage of Mama Barb's drunken Friday night stupor and shoved a handful of crack viles in his pocket along with three glocks. His addiction forced him to brag about what he stole and how "stupid," Mama Barb was for letting him in her apartment. Steven even had the nerve to smoke with the hood snitches and word got back to Rico in thirty minutes. That "hot" gossip blazed a trail throughout North Orange and that's how Steven became a wanted man.

Rico's house phone was wiretapped for the last six months and the feds knew that Steven would prove to be the fall guy in the operation. Alex had his own "fall" in mind. He was cool with Dominick, aka, Nick, the sneaky cop who smacked the knuckle heads around at basketball games and after school in the Valley. Since Steven bit into Nick's profits by stealing the weapons and drugs, Nick was ready to pay Rico a personal favor. Nick gave Alex the heads up since Steven was related to me. Alex acquiesced with silence and hence the job was given the green light. Alex's only request was that Nick kept Steven out of a body bag.

As the sun began to settle on Garvey, Nick went on to the roof and dragged Steven's cranked out frame to the eleventh floor. Nick ravaged Steven's knees with a Billy club and flipped him over for one good crack against his scull. After that, he hoisted his body head first into the garbage shoot for an eleven foot fall into the needle and roach ridden garbage heap. Luckily, the remnants of an old mattress broke his fall as an elderly woman lifted the wall shoot and screamed in horror. The paramedics took their time in attending to him. Two officers in quad one were injured and another in the main quad. By the time Steven's mangled body made it on a stretcher to North Orange Memorial Hospital, Steven was paralyzed from the neck down and lost his ability to speak.

Nick received a handsome reward, including a promotion to detective and an antique World War II starter pistol. The feds criminal wrap sheet on Steven's crime sprees in New York City and the surrounding areas of Essex were enough for the feds to close the investigation on Steven without question. After a fully executed warrant, no weapons could be found at Mrs. Viv's home. Mrs. Viv cursed the federal officers, but fed the local officers who had been kind to her over the years. As for Steven and Mrs. Viv, well she was happy just tending to her dear boy without the worry of his drug addictive ways. She lobbied hard to get him on permanent disability and Medicare without question or inquiry. After a month long stay in Kessler, the prodigal son returned home again to Mrs. Viv's loving arms as she fed him soft mash potatoes and his favorite cherry Kool-Aid.

My life would never be the same again. Rumors of the shake down in North Orange ran rampant in three towns and followed me everywhere I went. My final resolve was to empty out my locker at St. James and remove all the left over clothes I left at Candy's house. Candy's analysis was simple, "Fuck em,' you know people only care about themselves at the end of the day. Besides, even if Alex had anything to do with it, you're his wife and you need to stay by his side even when things get rough."

As crazy as it sounded, for now, all I needed to do was to stay calm for the baby and keep Alex happy. That felt a lot better than my regrettable past.

That's Life

Mrs. Viv expected sympathy when she called to tell me about Steven's "terrible accident." I was more worried about what was taking Alex so long to get home because it was already nine thirty p.m.

"Mama, I'll call you later, it's Alex."

When I reached the door, Alex walked in with beer on his breath smiling. He wasn't drunk, but he looked like he had a good time with somebody. I pushed him off me and said, "Where were you I was worried to death!"

He laughed and said, "Just celebrating with Jack, I'm sorry I forgot to call you baby."

I started to walk away as I tightened my robe around my stomach. He grabbed my arm and said, "C'mon now, Shanelle, don't be mad, you know this is not like me."

"You're damn right this is not you and I don't like it one bit Alex."

Alex started laughing as he began to take off his soiled clothes. He took off each piece and stated his intentions, "Feisty one huh? Didn't you forget I'm your husband, your lover, your savior, provider and daddy to our son, don't you forget that sweetie."

I didn't like his tone and said, "Sweetie my ass, sleep on the couch, you stink."

Alex dropped his hands to the side after his Billy Dee Williams act and said, "I'm going to take a shower and get into bed right next to my beautiful wife."

I took my robe off and laid it across the foot of the bed. Alex took a shower and started singing a Larry Graham

song as I rolled my eyes around in my head. I turned over
twice as my stomach hardened and settled down. Alex stood
at the sink and brushed his teeth. He came to the entrance of
the doorway with a mouth full of frothy toothpaste spit and
said, "You still love me right?"

I wanted to vomit at the sight of him, but he was too
charming. I put the covers over my head as he started
laughing. "I know you can't resist me girl." He went back
into the bathroom and began to gargle. When he walked
back into the room, Alex began to tease me by reciting the
poem I wrote for him on our honeymoon. He pulled the
sheet off me and threw it to the floor. "The maiden sighs
today, it burrows beneath her brow, he who ponders deadly
sacrifices, take a final bow."

I turned on my side and said, "Alex, you're drunk,
go to bed."

Alex slid next to me and put his arms around my
stomach and said, "Pumpy, mommy's mad at me, but she'll
forgive me, joy always comes just before dawn."

I ignored Alex and after a few tosses and turns I
finally went to sleep. There was so much confusion in the
things he said, I could hardly make sense of it all. I simply
decided to let it go for another day.

Special Delivery

I closed out the Fall semester with a B plus average. I signed up for two independent study classes for the spring which cut my commute down to one day per week. By the time March rolled around, with one more month to go, I was ready to pop. Alex was promoted to detective and received a nice raise. He was so diligent at saving his money, we were able to put a down payment on a three bedroom house in Brick, New Jersey. I spent most of my time shopping for the baby. The sky was the limit for Pumpy's nursery. Alex's mother damn near cashed in her pension to make sure Pumpy was set with every need and want. To prepare for Pumpy's arrival, Alex and I took a Lamaze class together with nine other couples. Alex made small talk with all the other men while I quietly listened to every word the instructor had to say. I wanted to make sure Pumpy's delivery was as smooth as possible. I also registered for a breast feeding class. Alex threw his hands up at the idea but wanted me to nurse just the same. We went to the Fosters for dinner three times a week and walked the boardwalk at night to keep my body in shape. I was so amazed at the life inside of me, my weight issues simply drifted away.

Alex and I went to my last dr.'s appointment together. He hung on every word Dr. Robinson said regarding labor and delivery. He was poised and in control as she gave him last minute instructions.

"You don't have to rush to the hospital the minute you feel contractions Shanelle. I would like you to bare with the pain as much as you can and call me when the contractions are at least fifteen minutes apart. The baby is in position. He's going to come when he's good and ready so be patient with him and be patient with each other."

By the time April 1st arrived, I completed my classes and bunkered down for Pumpy's arrival. I spent most of my time nesting in various ways. I tested the rocking chair, double checked the harness points on the car seat and dusted the blinds. Mrs. Viv called intermittently to check on me. She was so busy taking care of Steven's acute care status, she barely had time to talk. When she did call, she bragged about his accomplishments like he was a new born.

"Today Steven said, 'Ahhh, ahhh', for the first time Shanelle. I was so tickled pink I had to write it in my diary."

"That's nice Mama," I replied. Deep in the crevice of my brain, I remembered when Steven used to heckle at mentally handicap people. I smirked to myself thinking, "Karma is a bitch."

"Girl, Steven made a big stink on himself today. It was so bad, I had to call the aid to help me."

"Wow," I thought. "Instead of him smearing it on the walls, it can finally reach the toilet bowls."

"Listen mama, I've gotta go, I'm going to the Fosters tonight for dinner. It's family night and I don't want to be late."

There was a long pause in the phone. Mrs. Viv began to cry and said, "Look at me carrying on about Steven and here you are getting ready to have my first grandson, how selfish of me. Are you ready for all of this Shanelle?"

I rolled my eyes up in the air at her question. Back in the day, if she would have seen me roll my eyes, I would have been sent flying across the room. I made another resolve about my mother, she wasn't going to change,

Steven was her life and that was that. So, even if Pumpy had to sleep in a drawer, she would never know the wiser.

"Sure mama, we're ready, I have a wonderful husband and we're going to be great parents."

Avoidance on her part came quickly. "Well would you look at the time, I have to feed Steven now. Take care Shanelle."

I didn't even say goodbye. I hung up the phone and immediately rubbed my stomach.

"Oh Pumpy, your granny is a piece of work. We won't try to change her though, she has to do that on her own."

As time marched on, it became more and more difficult to get around. Alex wanted to make us more comfortable so he traded in his Mazda and we bought a red Jeep Cherokee. I was thrilled because it was just enough room to stretch out for the three of us. Alex took me for a ride to the beach after we left the dealership and headed for the beach. It was a chilly day, but the warm sun felt so good against my face, I begged Alex to walk with me along the shore line. I waddled around for a little while, but the false contractions got so intense we had to sit down. Alex sat behind me as we practiced breathing together. He rubbed my legs down as we reminisced about all the days we spent on the beach together. Dusk began to settle on the sky as Alex held me in his arms. The water was so enchanting that I didn't want to leave with the exception of the cold wind. Alex got up and extended his hand to help me up. When he did, there was a sudden pop between my legs. If felt like someone popped a champagne cork inside of me. Suddenly, a huge splash of water crashed between my legs like a busted water balloon. I got so nervous I screamed, "Alex, I broke something." Alex looked down at my legs and said, "Shanelle, your water just broke." The sweet and pungent odor whipped through the wind and into my nostrils. My face scoured up but I remembered thinking how good it felt to get all of that water out of me. Fluid continued to trickle down my leg as Alex said, "Damn, the jeep." I gave him a look like, "Don't you start." Alex started smiling and said, "Take off your pants."

I looked around. The coast was clear. I held onto Alex's back as he peeled the fluid ridden pants off my legs. He turned them inside out and wiped the excess off my legs with the driest part of the material. Suddenly, a numbing pain shot through my back. The pain spiraled up into a tight ball and landed in my stomach in sharp agonizing pain. I bent over thinking the pain would quickly subside but it got worse as I stood straight up and held my stomach.

"Ohhhh, Alex! It hurts, it hurts, help me."

Alex put his arm around my waist and said, "I know baby, it's a contraction, remember?"

Fear overwhelmed me as I looked back at the crashing waters and contemplated running into the ocean. Maybe a large whale could swallow me whole and put me out of my misery. Alex had other plans.

"C'mon Shanelle, you can do it mommy, let's get to the car."

The pain started to subside as we walked back to the Jeep. Alex made me wait on the side walk while he covered up his precious passenger seat with anything he could find.

"Alex!" I shouted, "They're leather seats, let me get in!" Alex looked at the amniotic fluid trickling down my leg and said, "You're right, I'm sorry."

It didn't matter what I said, he didn't want it on his precious seats. He grabbed the paper mats off the floor and placed them on the seat. Alex hoisted me on to the crumbled paper like a senior citizen sitting in three layers of diapers. I rolled my eyes at him as he walked around the front of the car.

He started up the car and said, "Ok, let's get you home."

"Home?" I asked, "Take me to the hospital now!"

Alex looked at me like I forgot every labor and delivery rule written for mankind. "Shanelle, the doctor said…"

I immediately interrupted him and said, "Doctor this, doctor that, it's not what she says, this shit hurts!" Suddenly a sharp pain shot into my pelvic area again as I screamed, "Help, oohh, help me, I can't take this!"

Alex took off down the street like he was kidnapping me. "Shanelle," Alex replied, "Your contractions are twenty minutes apart, I just timed them, we have to go home first."

I held the bottom of my stomach and growled like a demonic pit bull.

"Take me to the hospital now."

Alex couldn't resist. He started laughing and said, "Ok, I'm sorry, I'll take you now."

After a quick check by calm and cool Dr. Robinson, she sent me back home to ride it out.

"Shanelle, listen to me, you can do this, you haven't even dilated yet. Go home and walk around. Call me when the contractions are ten minutes apart."

I cried all the way home. There was nothing that Alex could say or do to console me. He got so nervous he drove to his mother's house to help him get through the ordeal. I stayed in the car and damned them to a life of misery.

"I'm not going to make love to Alex again. He better not come near me or I swear I'll cut him!"

Another sharp pain shot through me as Mrs. Foster scurried out of the house, happy and calm.

"Are you having a contraction Shanelle?"

"Yes!" I screamed.

"Shanelle, look at me baby and focus."

She reclined the seat and held on to it so it wouldn't jerk back. Mrs. Foster grabbed my hand and said, "Look at the ceiling baby and focus, focus, that's a girl, you can do it."

Her voice was so soothing and calm that I was able to settle down. Alex breathed a sigh of relief as he helped his mother get in the back seat.

Three hard contractions came in the time it took to get home. Mrs. Foster was consistent in getting me through each one as Alex nervously patted my hand.

Once we reached home, Mrs. Foster escorted me to the shower for a quick wash up. Alex packed the car with my bag and Pumpy's car seat. The contractions became more and more intense as I cried to the heavens in doubt.

"Please help me, I can't do this God."

"Ok Shanelle," Mrs. Foster softly replied. "You can do this child, look at me and focus baby."

Alex laid my clothes out while Mrs. Foster helped me towel off. My compassion for others kicked in when the contractions stopped. I hugged Alex and apologized for yelling at him. Another contraction came and I damned his existence again. "Oh God, this was all your idea, you should be having Pumpy not me!"

Alex ignored me as he looked at his watch. "Mom, it's time to go, their fifteen minutes apart."

"Who am I chop liver?" I asked. "I'm the one having this baby!" The two of them coaxed me through my tirade. "You're right Shanelle, you are certainly right, are you ready?" Alex asked.

"Yes, I'm ready."

They put me in the back of the car like I was a criminal. I guess it looked too embarrassing riding in the front seat thrashing my head around like a crazy person.

The pain was so intense, I put my foot against the

rear window of the driver's side and called on all of my biblical heroes. "Moses, Matthew, Luke, John, Joseph, please deliver me." Mrs. Foster looked at Alex and said, "She's rolling some serious holy dice for this delivery."

I didn't find a damn thing funny and neither did Alex when he saw my filthy sneaker resting on his precious window.

"Shanelle, take your foot down."

"Shut up Alex!" I screamed, as I held on to my hard belly.

Alex cocked his neck to the left and turned on the radio. I knew he didn't like that comment, but for the moment, I didn't care. As we rolled into the emergency entrance, I grabbed Mrs. Foster's sweat jacket and covered my face. The emergency room nurse met us at the car and tapped on my window. Alex jumped out and held the door open for her as he grabbed my hand.

A gentle voice said, "Well, well, who do we have here, a celebrity? Why are you hiding your face?" I took the sweatshirt off my face and cried like an episode out of I Love Lucy.

"I'm having a baby and I don't want to do this." She was sympathetic to my cause, but a smart ass in the same breath.

"Oh dear, I'm sorry sweetie, you made your bed, now you have to…"

"Don't even go there Nurse Ratchet!" I replied. "You don't even know me!"

The seemingly kind nurse looked at Alex and said, "Feisty one, good thing there's a shift change in fifteen minutes."

Alex nodded in agreement as I sat in the wheel chair. They wheeled me down the longest hallway of my life. The nurse parked me next to a small window while a frail woman asked for our insurance cards.

"Excuse me," I said. "I really need something for the pain."

The small woman barely looked up and said, "I know sweetheart, your doctor will help you."

Alex put his hand on my shoulder and said, "Hang in there babe, we'll be upstairs soon."

After the paperwork, insurance and request for my own room was complete, an orderly took us upstairs to labor and delivery. Another nurse escorted us to a smaller room with two chairs and a hospital bed. She handed me a plastic bag with my name on it and said, "You can put your belongings in here and give them to your husband to take home. In the meantime, you can disrobe and put a gown on for me. We're going to hook you up to a machine to monitor your baby's vital signs." I started crying as my world became someone else's. The nurse gave me a hug and said, "I know sweetie, this is your first, it's okay to be a little scared, but you'll be fine, you're in good hands."

I looked at her with the saddest eyes and said, "Can I leave my socks on, my feet are cold?"

The nurse went to a small cabinet and pulled out a pair of socks with grips on the bottom. "Here," she said. "Put these on, the doctor's going to let you walk the hallway for a while to get through some of your contractions."

Mrs. Foster and Alex sat upright and attentive as they watched my every move. Alex was more than happy to get a break from my dramatic tirades back at the house.

I went into the small bathroom and changed into my gown. All I could do was hold onto the bottom of my belly and pray to God for forgiveness. My back was throbbing and the cramping intensified with each labor pain. "Alex!" I screamed. "Here comes another one!"

He came into the bathroom and wrapped his arms around me as I hugged him back. As the contraction deepened into a painful swell, Alex rubbed the lower portion of my back with hard strokes.

"Breathe Shanelle, that's it breathe."

"It hurts."

"I'm sorry it hurts baby, but you can do it Shanelle, just breathe."

I wanted to collapse to the ground, but Alex was strong enough to hold me up. After the pain subsided, we walked back into the waiting area. The nurse took me by wheelchair to my private room. The minute Alex opened the door, I began to relax. The room was decorated with soft hues of blue and swirled into paisley prints. The nurse told us that we would spend most of our time in our "labor," room until I reached ten centimeters. Alex shook his head with nervous confidence as he patted my swollen hands. Another nurse walked in with medical machinery, including an intravenous drip. They poked, prodded and taped me up like an old shirt hanging on a clothes line. The next contraction came with so much intensity, the nurses had to wait for me to ride it out. I begged for mercy and forgiveness.

"Please nurse Carol, call my doctor and tell her to give me something, I can't take it!" By this time, even Alex felt sorry for me.

"Yes, please call her, she needs something." Just then, a resident came in to monitor my progress. He was five feet tall and less than a buck-o-five. As he introduced himself, I quickly wrote him off as useless simply because he didn't have any medicine.

"I don't mean to be rude, but what are you going to do?" I asked. The small young man smiled and said, "I'm going to see how much you dilated." Then he climbed on my bed. With rubber gloves on his hands, he exposed his tiny toothpick fingers to check me. I immediately clamped my legs down and said, "No way, I want a female resident." Besides, he was so tiny, I thought I was going to swallow him whole. Another contraction came and I began to cry. "Please, Moses, Aaron, Joseph, help me Jesus!"

Mrs. Foster patted my head with a washcloth and said, "I was wondering when you were going to ask for Him." Luckily, the little resident didn't get offended. In two seconds, Dr. Robinson arrived and I finally felt relieved.

"Doc, you gotta help me!" I said. My hands reached out for her and she grabbed them with a warm and caring smile.

"Ok Shanelle, settle down. Is your contraction over?"

"Yes I whimpered."

"Ok, let me check you and we'll see what we can do about the pain."

She checked my cervix and said, "Sorry Shanelle, you're only dilated two centimeters, let's hold off on pain medication for an hour."

I immediately started crying as Alex rubbed my back. She looked at me with concern in her eyes and said, "I'm going to take a nap because I just finished a cesarean section then you can have all of my attention, ok?" She held my trembling hand and wiped my face. "You'll be fine, your little one likes it in there, but we'll see him in due time."

I began to cry harder when she walked out. Even with Alex and his mother there, I felt abandoned. I was yearning for my mother to tell me it was going to be all right. Alex ran his fingers through my hair as the tears ran down my cheek. His hand got tangled in a ferocious knot as my head jerked back.

"Ow, that hurts Alex!" As hard as he was trying, I knew he had enough of me and I damn sure had enough of him. Sheer vengeance seeped into my blood stream as the handsome wonder stood next to me free from agonizing pain. As another labor pain kicked in, I looked at him and thought, "That leather seat incident is going to cost you a few lonely nights." Mom Foster must have seen steam rising from out of my scalp. She immediately jumped in.

"Alex, why don't you take a break while I sit with Shanelle. Go get some coffee son, she'll be fine."

I rubbed my scalp so he could remember the pain he inflicted on me. Alex winked at me with his cocky ass and walked out. He didn't even ask me if I wanted anything. It only made me take out another "pay back is a bitch," card and add it to my deck.

As for Mom Foster, she decided to do a little soul searching on me. She turned around twice to make sure Alex was out of ear shot and said, "Shanelle, I never got a chance to talk to you about what happened between Alex and I so long ago." She grabbed my hand as I grimaced in pain. The pain in my stomach didn't stir up any empathy in me. The fact that I needed her by my side forced me to listen.

"That was a terrible thing that happened that night and as a mother, there is nothing you won't do for your son."

I looked into her eyes and could see the eyes of my mother speaking to me.

"The love between a mother and a son can be the most magical feeling on earth. At times I think there is nothing that I wouldn't do for him. I ask God to forgive me every night for what I put my poor son through. I don't know if I will be forgiven, but in the meantime, I will be there for him until my dying day." Even though her speech did not sound rehearsed, Alex made similar promises to me. I wondered if they rehearsed their speeches together.

Mrs. Foster wrapped her arms around me and stroked my back in downward motions as I strained and gritted my teeth. The contractions were becoming more and more intense as time went by. If the pain of labor had anything to do with my past sins and regression, I surely needed God to forgive me. Once the contraction subsided, I leaned back into the pillows while Mom Foster fed me ice chips. Alex returned to the room with Dr. Robinson. She checked me again and to my surprise, I dilated to four centimeters.

"Good girl Shanelle, you're making good progress! Just get to five centimeters and when you do I will authorize an epidural to relieve some of the pain."

I think I passed out five times to catch a nap between contractions. After one full hour, a team of residents came to check on me. They gathered around me as the anesthesiologist explained the process of inserting a sixty-foot needle into my spine to temporarily paralyze me so I wouldn't feel the pain or something. It all sounded like, "Blah, blah, blah, consent form, sign here, blah, blah, blah."

"Yeah, yeah, go ahead, do it doc, I'm ready and I also need to go to the bathroom."

One of the male residents failed to exercise one of his Hippocratic Oaths and began to laugh at my agonizing state of mind. I gave him the evil eye and said, "What's so funny, me, or that stain on your shirt? Did your mother forget to put your bib on today?" The female residents rallied around me and laughed while the guys held it in. Mrs. Foster made excuses for me as Alex gave me a high five. The need to go to the bathroom suddenly overwhelmed me as I explained my situation to the nurse. The nurse replied, "Honey you have a catheter on, do you feel like you're going to pass your bowels?" She asked.

I thought to myself, *"No nurse Ratchet number two, I need to take a shit!"*

Without further hesitation, four interns passed me onto another bed and shipped me off to delivery. Alex donned a green surgical suit. He hugged his mother as they said a quick prayer for me and Pumpy.

I began to strain and push but the nurses stopped me. "No, no honey, don't push yet!"

I tried to resist the urge to push as they wheeled me into an extremely cold operating room. It was so medicinal I felt like I was the bride of Frankenstein. I was in good company too. Alex stood next to me wearing throw up green with his hands across his chest in bouncer mode waiting for his precious Pumpy to be born.

They gathered around me as Dr. Robinson took position and gave instructions to Alex. Alex held my legs up on one side as the other nurse stood on the opposite side.

"Ok Shanelle, take one deep breath and push for me."

I did what she said and immediately stopped as the sound of chicken necks stuck in a grinding machine filled my entire existence. "I can't, he's breaking me!" Alex went into football mode and began to coach me.

"Ok babe, let's make this quick, you can do it. Listen to the doctor. Take a deep breath and push, I'm right here." The tone in his voice was calm as I took a deep breath and pushed. My response was deafening as the pressure from Pumpy's head ripped me from front to back.

"I see the head, good girl Shanelle! Take a deep breath and do it again."

Alex held my hand as he began to sweat. He looked back at me and pushed my legs back as I pushed again.

"Quick, quick Shanelle, here comes the shoulders… you can do it."

More chicken necks snapped as I looked at Alex for motivation. One last hard push came as Alex eyes widened in pure delight. My head slumped onto the pillow with relief as Pumpy finally came out in eight pounds and nine ounces of pure magical joy!

Alex dropped to his knees and lifted his hands to heaven as Dr. Robinson announced, "It's a boy! It's a boy!"

She held Pumpy up for me to see. Pumpy quivered up his lips and cried out loud. After that, we all started crying. I was the first one to gain composure and talk to him. As the nurses attended to him he began to settle down just by the sound of my voice. I was amazed at his sheer size. He had a big Charlie Brown head, massive hands and broad shoulders like his father. In fact, everything seemed to emulate the Foster family tree. I looked to the side as Alex stood up over me and planted what seemed like fourteen peanut butter breath kisses on my puffy cheeks. Suddenly more cramping followed as Dr. Robinson pressed down on my stomach and delivered the placenta. I tried to keep my head up to see all the commotion, but I was too exhausted. Alex walked over to the attending pediatrician and asked, "Ten fingers, ten toes?" The pediatrician laughed and said, "Yes, Mr. Foster." Alex continued his inventory like Pumpy was a race car.

"Penis?"

"Check."

"Hearing?" he asked.

"Looks good, he's following your voice right now."

Alex bent down in sheer wonderment and said, "Hello Pumpy, it's me Daddy." Pumpy let out a funny noise like he was a little Billy goat. The bond began right there as the pediatrician passed our little bundle to Alex.

Alex cried tears of joy as he held Pumpy for the first time. "Hey Pumpy, I would take you fishing but someone wants to meet you."

I held out my hands as Alex placed him in my arms. Pumpy was alert as he looked at his daddy towering over me.

Dr. Robinson and the attending pediatrician encouraged me to put Pumpy on my breast to nurse for a few minutes. My breasts looked too big for his mouth, but as Alex and Dr. Robinson exposed my breast to him, Pumpy immediately started thrashing his face back and forth to find me like a little pup. He opened his mouth and immediately latched on. Dr. Robinson stroked the side of his cheek as he began to suck. As the tears flowed down my cheek I thought to myself, "Mrs. Foster was right, it is magical." An instant bond came between us as I talked to my son. Alex stroked my hair line and cried some too. The two minute ordeal put Pumpy to sleep in an instant as they tucked him into his bassinet and put an i.d. bracelet on him to match mine. Alex turned to the pediatrician and said, "So doc, when does he go for the big snip?"

He tugged at his stethoscope and said, "Probably tomorrow, around ten."

Alex shook hands with him and said, "Do the right thing doc, just do the right thing."

He smiled and said, "Don't worry, it will be perfect."

Alex breathed a sigh of relief as we were ushered out of surgery and into my hospital room. Our new life with Pumpy had just begun.

Happily Ever After?

On day three of my hospital stay, we left in a balloon and flower trail of glory. Pumpy was officially named Troy Alexander Foster, but we still called him Pumpy. Mrs. Foster trailed behind us as Alex cursed every driver on the road.

"Slow down you idiot, we have a baby."

I looked at Alex like he was crazy. Suddenly everyone was a nut and idiot just because of his son. I sat in the back with Pumpy at Alex's request. It seemed that I was more calm then he was. Alex was determined to keep me home with him and I didn't mind because I wanted Pumpy to have a healthy start.

When we got home, there were boxes of pampers, gifts, flower arrangements and money envelopes waiting for us. I held Pumpy in my arms and went straight upstairs to his Noah's Ark nursery. Alex peeked in on us as I immediately went to the rocking chair and nursed him. He was always hungry. Pumpy would suck hard for five good minutes and then pass out like I slipped him a Mickey. While he was sleeping, I carefully changed the dressing from his circumcision and changed his pamper. Swaddling was his all time favorite as I laid him in his bassinet for the first time. Mrs. Foster peeked in but kept her distance. They were giving me just the right space to be with my son. The smell of chicken soup drifted into the room as I turned on his nursery monitor. Afterwards, I joined them downstairs for something to eat.

Mrs. Foster put a hot bowl of chicken soup on the

table for me as I sat down.

"It smells wonderful," I said.

Alex kissed my cheek and said, "You're doing a wonderful job mommy." I grabbed his wrist to make the feeling last a little longer and said, "Thank you, I needed to hear that."

I stayed with Alex and Mrs. Foster for a few minutes. Even though the nursery monitor was on, I wanted to check on Pumpy. I quietly slipped upstairs under the watchful eye of Alex. When I reached upstairs, my breasts began to leak the closer I got to his nursery. I stuck my head in the bassinet to listen to him breathing. He looked so peaceful tucked away in his quiet existence. Weariness began to set in as I sat in my rocking chair thinking about the world around me. Having Pumpy was Alex's greatest joy. Giving birth to him aroused feelings of motherhood, but not blissful happiness. My eyes began to soften as I searched for answers in my thoughts. The window facing me stirred up feelings of loneliness and sorrow as a soft rain began to fall. Tears falling down my cheek accompanied the orchestra outside as I quickly jotted a poem in Pumpy's baby book.

Rainy Days

The search outside my window
Offers no purpose to my refrain.
A spring breeze gracefully pirouettes
as I watch the pouring rain.
I hope the rain cleanses me
while falling softly to the left.
An innocent redemption,
Placed inside a delicate nest.
Upon the highest mountain,
welcome to the lair.

Delicate thoughts of your touch,
Breathlessly awaiting innocent air.
Focus on reflection,
will it ever be explained?
Let it happen naturally,
Find solace in my refrain.

Alex stood in the doorway watching me wipe my tears away as I closed Pumpy's baby book. He knelt down in front of me and placed his head in my lap. He looked so humble as if he was a peasant before my throne. Reality offered a different conclusion. In my weakest hour, Alex swept me off my feet and defined the person I had become. There was no way I could abandon the notion of being a good mother to his son. I wanted the same things, but it was much too soon. I was also unsure of what price I would have to pay. Our little miracle was Alex's sweetest redemption. My mind, heart and womb was the place that cultivated Alex's grand scheme. For this, my life needed to be put on hold. I needed Alex's support in being a good husband and father. Deep inside, I knew I had a greater destiny. The temper festering inside of him needed to stay there while I figured a way out. I began to close my eyes as I stroked Alex's head. He nestled his cinnamon face in my lap and squeezed me tight as Pumpy began to stir. The sound of a faint whimper forced Alex to his feet to fetch his son. He quickly picked him up and held him up to his face as he spoke to his little miracle.

"Hey little man, you hungry?" Alex laid him on the changing table and carefully changed his diaper. Pumpy's chubby legs jerked back as the cold air hit his bare skin. Pumpy began to pee but Alex was ready for him. "C'mon son, that old trick, I was ready for you." Alex wiped him down and carried him to me as I lifted up my shirt to nurse him. He grabbed his camera and began to take pictures of his son's first day home. The phone rang, but Mrs. Foster picked it up and received our congratulations from the well wisher. Pumpy nursed for six straight minutes and went right back to sleep. The classes on breastfeeding were so helpful to me that I knew my son was on the right track. Eat, poop and sleep was all he needed in his quaint routine. I looked up at Alex and thanked him. He was destined to be a good father and by the looks of things, as long as I stayed routine, he was definitely going to help me get strong again. Alex turned on a lullaby and tucked Pumpy back into his bassinet as I walked to our bedroom. I climbed into bed from sheer exhaustion as Alex tucked me in and kissed my forehead. Life stood still as I looked out the window. The clean air whipped under the window sill and forced fresh air into my nostrils just like my poem. I quietly closed my eyes and let the serenity of the moment claim me as I went to sleep. Taking each moment step by step was my resolve as I settled in Alex's and Pumpy's world.

Joy at Dawn

The smell of eggs and bacon woke me up as I rolled over and stretched. Pumpy's bassinet was right beside me. Luckily he started off on the right foot. I had to wake up twice for a feeding and he slept the night away like a good baby should. Alex was next to me as I looked at the clock. He rolled over and replied, "I'm off today, ma's downstairs cooking breakfast if you're hungry."

I took a slow walk to the shower and looked at my naked frame in the mirror. I must have been full of water weight, because I could immediately see a difference in weight loss. A soft smile escaped me as I looked in the mirror over the sink. No voices became me as I slowly brushed my teeth. I stepped into the shower and carefully washed my raw and achy frame. Parts of me felt alive and other parts of me felt like jello. I convinced myself that I was healing and that it was natural to feel that way. After I got dressed I joined Mrs. Foster in the kitchen.

"Good morning Shanelle, how did you sleep?"

"Great, Troy only woke up twice and went right back down after Alex changed his pamper."

"Good!" she replied. "Magical isn't it?"

We gave each other a toast as I replied, "Very magical."

Just then the doorbell rang. Mrs. Foster got up to answer it as I slowly began to eat. The excitement in Mrs. Foster's voice was a sure fire sign that Tammy was home from college and she had company.

"Nikki, so nice to meet you, Shanelle's in the

kitchen, come on in."

Shock overwhelmed me as I stood up to greet Tammy and Nikki, Rico's sister from Garvey. In an instant, I knew I was in big trouble. Nikki and Tammy hugged me as I looked at Nikki and said, "What brings you here?" Tammy and Nikki stared at each other and began to laugh. The quick glance between them wasn't a girlfriend glance, it looked a little more intimate.

"Oh, Tammy and I are hanging out during the break. Besides I'm kinda in between housing right now."

No doubt she was. The feds hauled Rico and the rest of her drug smuggling family out of Garvey so fast there was no way she had time to recover her things. The New York Times did a full expose on the reputed family and standing in my kitchen was the good black sheep of the family. The sound of Alex's voice sent me flying out of my skin as he beckoned me.

"Shanelle!" he said. "Troy is up and I'm sure he's hungry."

I tucked my robe into my body and grabbed a slice of cantaloupe as I headed upstairs. Alex flew down the stairs so fast he almost knocked me down. I held on to the banister to brace my fall and to listen to his tirade. The confusion and arguing ensued the minute I reached the top landing.

"Who do you think you are Alex, I came to see my nephew and Nikki has known Shanelle since high school!"

I picked Pumpy up and settled his cries as he latched onto my breast.

"Tammy," Alex said, you've got a lot to learn. I'm sorry Nikki, being here is a conflict of interest and you're smart enough to know why. So now that you know who I am, I'm going to have to ask you to leave."

Mrs. Foster jumped in as I rocked Troy back and forth while he quietly suckled.

"No ma, that's not an option either. Not my house or your house!" Alex shouted.

The front door slammed as I stood at the window burping Pumpy. Small circular rubs forced a small burp up as he held his head up alert and attuned.

Tammy stormed down the walkway holding Nikki's hand as they walked to the car. Before she got in she looked up at my window. I smiled as a quiet tear trickled down my chin and into the burping cloth. I raised my hand and gave her the peace sign as she quickly reciprocated with a smile. "At least you're free Tammy," I thought. I would have given anything to jump in the car and ride off into the sunset. Like anything else in my life, it was a dream deferred as Pumpy cooed in my ear. It was the sweetest sound imaginable as I sat down again to take the pressure off my stomach. I sang a little Chaka melody to him just like I used to sing when I was heart sick for Derrick. *"I will love you anyway, even if you cannot stay…"* I quietly wished it away as Alex stood in the doorway like nothing happened.

"Tammy's upset, but I can't jeopardize our safety."

I nodded in agreement as I handed Troy to Alex.

"Hey man," Alex said, as he lifted Troy to the sky and thanked the almighty for his healthy son."

Troy's reflexes quickly forced his arms to reach out as Alex held him up and then slowly back down again. Worry never became me. I knew that Alex would give his very life for the both of us. Alex pulled him into his chest as I gently rocked back and forth. He quietly looked at me and said, "I love you Shanelle, if I haven't said it enough." I turned my thoughts to the window and tucked the smallest piece of strand behind my ear and said, "I love you too."

Fly Away

Four months quickly passed us by as Troy grew by leaps and bounds. Alex and I competed against each other by capturing the most precious pictures on film of our pride and joy. Troy was the chunkiest baby in South Jersey and every beach comber and well wisher stopped us to admire him. In fact, nursing him throughout those early months, brought my shape right back to regular size to Alex's delight. The appeal of my premarital weight enticed Alex every night, but we only averaged three times a week. One good thing about our little Troy was his need to get in between us. Alex adored him, but called him a cock blocker just the same. I immediately began taking birth control pills and worked out feverishly to combat any extra weight gain. Candy came to visit us three times since his birth as she began to plan her wedding with Clinton. She was the only friend I had and the only friend that Alex accepted in our quiet life. It was a great relief having her around as we talked about her fashion layout for the upcoming nuptials planned for the spring.

Calls from home were far and between as Mrs. Viv tended to her own newborn. Steven made very little progress except for pulling on the phone cord when she called me. My life was so busy tending to our son and Alex's need, forgiveness was sweet and avoidance was a must.

On a bright spring day just before dawn, we drove out to the beach to take a morning stroll. The view on the beach was spectacular as an orange sun began to rise above the ocean. Alex wrapped us tight in his arms as Troy pulled at my shirt happily nursing at my breast. His fat chunky feet sat in Alex's mouth as Troy laughed in between sucking.

"It can't get any better than this Shanelle," Alex said, as he kissed my neck.

I took Troy off my breast, kissed his cheek and handed him to Alex. "I guess you could say that Alex," I replied, as I tucked my son's food supply back into my sports bra and walked closer to the shore line.

I watched the sunrise against the backdrop of my husband and son. Alex loved this time of day because of the glorious view the sun provided every morning. Thinking about it made me fold my arms across my chest as I began to think about my future. The majestic ocean has a way of broadening ideas. It certainly had that affect on me the day I laid eyes on Alex and the on the night we were reintroduced after three years. Alex broke my virginity, put a ring on my finger, claimed me as his wife and mother to his precious son. Thinking about the experience said very little about who I really was. There were two opportunities in my life that needed to be completed. Finishing college was one and exploring my career interests. Writing felt so good to me especially if it dealt with children's rights. I rubbed my arms up and down to ward off the morning chill as I contemplated St. James and my transfer to Monmouth University. An internship in Washington still appealed to me as the greatest dream deferred. Looking back at Alex bonding with Troy offered little hope of how I could make it to Washington, but I was determined to find my way. I needed to get organized again to determine my future. "Funny," I thought, as the waves crashed upon shore. I learned that bit of advice from the great Alex, himself. I looked back one last time as he poked and prodded at Pumpy's fat belly and chunky toes. A few birds flew by over the vast ocean prompting me to put a few things in perspective. "This butterfly needs to spread her wings and fly."

Stay tuned...

"Love's Twilight" is the climatic ending to Moody's three part trilogy, Wild Innocence, a Tale from the Eighties and Sweet Redemption, the sequel.

Love, seduction and murder finds Shanelle gripped with confusion and doubt as a brief encounter with Derrick tests her devotion to Alex. While Shanelle begins to question his integrity as a police officer, Rico orders a ruthless "hit" for the narcotics and weapons seizure at the Garvey Projects. Shanelle's life quickly unravels as a childhood truth is revealed, leaving her no choice but to stand tall and finally embrace self love.

When you close this book, please be encouraged to email me online at moody@moodyholiday.com or visit my website at www.moodyholiday.com. I would love to read your thoughts, wishes, hopes and dreams. Thank you.

Acknowledgements

My heartfelt thanks goes out to all the people who supported the release of *Wild Innocence, A Tale from the Eighties*.

To the staff at Nibiru's; Rafiyq, Ranisha, Chonna, Tyisha and Darnell, thank you for your endless support.

Special thanks to Roy W., better days will follow. Thank you.

www.moodyholiday.com